Those Necessary Thorns

Desiree Elizabeth Taylor

Sabrina Childress

First Edition: December 2012

Printed in the United States of America

ISBN: 978-0-615-78860-9

ACKNOWLEDGEMENTS

"because of these surpassingly great revelations. Therefore, to keep me from becoming conceited, I was given a thorn in my flesh, a messenger of Satan, to torment me. Three times I pleaded with the Lord to take it away from me." (2 Corinthians 12: 6-10)

A rose is….It blooms and dies and always blooms again. This, my first book, is dedicated to my husband Alfred, my cousins; LaQuita, Jessica, Janesha, and Chanel. My sisters Nina, Katrina, Tina, Arnetta, Charkina and Adriane. My mom; Deborah Jung. My favorite aunt Beverly Childress. My girls; Tiara, Jennifer, Marianne, Kimmie, and Jessica. My friend Brandon Moore, You can do it, dude! My creative soul mate George Burton. The greatest professor and friend to ever walk the earth, Donald Crumbley, and the always beautiful Sheila Carter. And to my Godmother Cheryl Anderson, for standing in the gap.

Enormous thanks to all who are reading this acknowledgment, and will call me later to ask why I didn't mention them. No worries, I'm protecting you. You're welcome!

There are people in my life that keep me from being conceited. They are the thorns that remind me that we have a purpose and a promise, and I intended to keep mine. I'm happy! I found my sexy.

CONTENTS

Acknowledgments

Those Necessary Thorns Desiree Elizabeth Taylor

THANK YOU!

THOSE NECESSARY THORNS

DESIREE ELIZABETH TAYLOR

BY

SABRINA CHILDRESS

MEET DESIREE
ELIZABETH TAYLOR

Meet Desiree Elizabeth Taylor aka Desi (Dez-ee) aka D.E.T. (Don't Even Think about it). She is African-American, tall (for a female) and medium build in her late twenties. She is a full figured woman with curves to die for and legs that should be insured for millions. She is all natural with medium length hair, brown eyes, dimples and a killer smile. She is "silly" in a sweet way and intelligent. She is judgmental – or so it appears – and serious while sympathetic and sincere.

Some would say she is wholesome – while others would gladly call her a bitch. She wears many 'hats' (as most women do), but her 'hats' bear the burden of those who look up to her, envy her and despise her.

She is married and is ALL things to her husband and half of all things (if not ALL things) to those around her. Always on public display, it is obvious that everyone examines her every move.

3

Even in the midst of such scrutiny she handles it with the grace of a lioness.

"She must be perfect" – or so they whisper in judgment. If only they knew or cared to engage her, they would undoubtedly become aware of her silent anguish. They would know she grew up not allowed to make the slightest of mistakes as this would mean to all those around her that she is, in fact, human and not infallible, therefore killing any hope those people ever had of the perfect woman being able to exist. But, this grooming made one thing certain for such a prodigy, Desiree was born to change the world – somehow – But how when women and men alike are intimidated simply by her presence?

She believes in GOD but feels like she let his calls go to voice mail or a cell phone ignore over the past few months. Desiree's story begins in a church on the first Sunday, better known as communion Sunday. The choir is singing, "It's Gonna Rain" by Rev. Milton and the Thompson Singers. As the selection ends the preacher takes to the pulpit to deliver his sermon about purpose and deliverance and willful sin. As she sits next to her husband at the family church where she grew up, she listens intently and looks around wondering if anyone can see the shame and guilt dripping from her ill spirit like a drain after a pouring rain.

The preacher commands the congregation with these words, "You knew what you were going to do before you did it. It didn't just happen. If you are anything like me, you planned it. You put it on your calendar or made a mental note. You even put things in place so that your plan would go uninterrupted." She mumbles a silent "I'm sorry" as tears start to well up in her eyes. Meanwhile, the congregation is in an uproar as the preacher continues.

"No one made you do it. You did it because you wanted to and you figured you'd ask for forgiveness later!"

"I'm sorry." Again she mumbles.

"Let your heart not be troubled sinner!" He stomps. "The Lord thy God has something greater for you. Cast your burdens on him and walk in your purpose!" The preacher screams. "Some of you even have your just in case he wants me to stay bag in your trunk right now! Let go of your wicked ways! They will keep you from the Kingdom of Heaven."

"This is too much to handle." Desi's heart starts to race. "I've got to get out of here." Posting up the black churches international symbol of "excuse me one second" she holds up her almighty index finger and steps lightly across the other church goers on her golden brown leather seated wooden pew. "I can't handle this." She couldn't stop sobbing and excused herself in a failed attempt to cover the turmoil brewing inside her with each word.

It seemed the combination of the Holy Ghost and the tall wooden oak vaulted cathedral ceilings and wide aisles were not enough to contain the volcano that was threatening to erupt inside Desiree. She made a mad dash for the sanctuary doors she swiped a few tissues from the box resting on the last pew, better known as the usher's row. The congregation was so involved in the preacher's words and the choir's rendition of the gospel song, "Make Me Over Again" that no one appeared to notice her sprinting through the foyer. Her heels made no sound as they barreled down the twelve maroon carpeted stairs. When she made it to the first corridor, she paused momentarily trying to determine whether to run out the double doors of the church or continue down the second flight of stairs to the women's bathroom in the basement of the church. *Bathroom*, she hastily decided to shake her head as if to snap out of a momentary lapse of insanity. With lightning speed, Desi found herself bounding down the steps two at a time until she heard the faint sound of her heels hitting the linoleum floor. She flung the door open, barely stepping inside before her silent tears became bursting uncontainable sobs and gasps.

Gripping the solid white walls on either side of her barely stable figure she inched her way into the safe haven away from the spectators and church-goers that would undoubtedly bombard her with unwanted questions and prayers. The click-clacking of her heels echoed through the short hallway adjoining the tan and white tiled floor that led to the open space between the sink and three stalls. Those white walls that felt safe just a moment ago started to simultaneously close in and swirl in a counter-clockwise motion around her. She fell forward on the white porcelain counter top knocking her knees against its wooden oak doors. *"Shit!"* It was all she could do to keep from fainting. Her head felt just as heavy as her heart. With one elbow on the sink and the other arm extended she slowly turned on the cold water. The cold splashes popped onto her features like hot grease. In slow motion, her hands came together to form a cup of sorts to carry the colder water from the faucet spout to her face. With her head tilted toward the ceiling and her eyes closed tight the water made contact. She allowed every single drop of life to inhale and exhale from her body. Her hands slid methodically down her cheeks, then her chin, and then her neck onto her shoulders and passed her breast and dropped like forty pound weights to her sides. Her breast were full of stress with each rise and fall as her breathing had become deliberate and labored causing her to swallow hard with each compression. She was drowning in her own tears.

Suddenly, she was awake. Fully. Honestly. Awake. Desi's eyes started to gradually open and the long thin white fluorescent lights affixed to the ceiling became clear. Now moaning through her tears, her head reluctantly starts the cautious climb forward. The enormous mirror directly in front of her anxiously awaited the reflection her shameful brown eyes, it was time to come clean with the woman in the mirror. Her naked eyelashes held big droplets of water that seemed to shine unsteadily as she blinked lethargically at her reflection. Disgusted, she turned away only to force her neck back to its original position. With square shoulders and flat palms against the counter top, she leans in for closer review of the turmoil in her face staring back at her. Her conscience would not let her run from it any longer. With tears still falling she bit her bottom lip and painfully remembered what brought her to this point.

THE MISTAKE

Earlier this year, my husband James ran into a woman. A woman that continually caused him to question every choice he'd ever made in life. She was classy, secure, smart and extremely plain. To J.J., that was an odd combination and that made her interesting. She wasn't school teacher sexy or even librarian plain, she was more of the nothing much to look at, wouldn't notice her in a crowd type of plain. Nothing like Desiree, everybody notices Desiree for one reason or another, even when they are trying not to. He sat next to her at a café near his office and she started a conversation with him about his choice of necktie. He smiled at the simplicity of her. As silly as it sounded, he was astonished by the way she would ask unsuspecting questions that would divulge more than he would ever voluntarily provide to any stranger. She learned almost everything there was to know about him in a week's time. Until one day, she asked, "Have you ever been kissed?"

"Excuse me?"

"You heard me."

"Yes. Yes, I did. Which is why you are getting the reaction you're getting."

"Answer the question Jones-y."

"Nicknames," He teased. "I didn't know we were on that level in our relationship."

"Guess that makes two of us because I didn't know we were in a relationship."

"Well played. Well played!"

"Now that we've got that settled answer my question."

"Of course I've been kissed. I'm married, remember." He said with a smile so wide his front teeth were visible.

"Yes, I do remember. But that doesn't mean you've ever *really* been kissed." She said stopping in front of him. They stood face to face with an inch of space between them. She kissed his bottom lip and held it. Every fiber of his body said to *push her away,* but he made no attempt. That was the moment she became, *'the mistake'.*

For weeks, he avoided the café. After working late one evening, he'd ordered delivery from the same café. Hours later he exited the building and there stood *'the mistake'.* He walked past as if she didn't exist and she followed begging him to acknowledge her. When he didn't, she told him that all she wanted was for someone to notice her. He'd instantly felt awful. That night, she played on his empathy and treated her to dinner and drinks. By the fourth bottle of Fitz Gewurztraminer wine, they were inebriated. One thing led to another and J.J. rented a room at the Renaissance Hotel and for the first time in his married life, made love to a woman that was not his wife. Once it was over, *'the mistake'* asked him to stay…he left. James felt sick to his stomach and raced home to me, his unsuspecting wife.

That night, when James walked through the door, I was in the kitchen putting away the dinner I cooked earlier in the evening. He came in quietly and helped me do the dishes.

"Hey you! How was your day?" I asked kissing his cheek.

"Fine," He said flatly.

"Tough one, huh?" I asked only slightly interested.

"No."

"Okay. I see someone isn't in a chatty mood tonight."

"Not really. How was your day?" He asked out of habit.

"Great! I've got two new clients and I've decided to get a new wardrobe. My closet is so boring." J.J. didn't respond. I wiped my hands and went upstairs. I figured he was too tired to talk and I was too excited about my professional victory and my new wardrobe to pay attention. James crawled into bed a few hours later after showing. I was half asleep but glanced at the clock on the nightstand. I could tell he wasn't resting well because he tossed and turned all night and when I tried to put my arms around him he moved away. I sat up and turned on the light.

"Do you want to talk about it, babe," I asked in the best girlfriend tone I could muster.

"Talk about what?" He said without turning around.

"The reason you are so agitated."

"I'm not. I'm just feeling funny."

"Are you sick?" I said touching his forehead with the back of my hand.

"No. I'm just in a weird way right now. When I figure it out, I will let you know." He snapped.

"Fine then! I don't know what your problem is but don't take it out on me James!" I pulled the covers over my head and tried to sleep with the unsettling feeling that started to stir inside me. In hindsight, I guess I should have paid more attention to it, but I didn't. Over the next few months, we would argue over the silliest things and makeup sex was not even an option. The more we fought, the more distant J.J. became. But somehow he always made sure to give me an event schedule for public appearances even though we were at war at home and I had no idea why.

That night, James made a personal promise to himself that he would never have sex again with anyone other than me. But he wasn't ready to let the relationship with *'the mistake'* go, he liked her too much. He continued to see *'the mistake'* on a regular basis.

THE GOOD, THE BAD, AND THE UGLY

Our towered Victorian home rested in the center of the block. The exterior was gray with maroon trim and the backyard was large enough for a seating area, garden and an oversized trampoline in the backyard. Since we were big kids at heart, we paid the previous owners a little extra to leave it there. We fell in love with it the moment we saw it! The porch was enclosed and wrapped around half the house. All the windows were oversized bay windows which allowed plenty of natural light throughout the house. Our driveway was long, wide, and made of maroon brick which led to a detached three car garage, complete with a guest house on top. It was small and reminded me of a tree house.

Thanks to the wonderful man that gets to call himself my husband, Mr. James Jones Taylor or J.J., for the past four years I've enjoyed every moment of being the independent, happily married woman that I am today. When I stood in front of my family and friends on our wedding day and pledged my love and allegiance to his six foot, two inches of mulatto manliness I felt him tremble. In front of all those witnesses he said, "It's amazing how I'm standing here, holding my wife's hands, looking like a rock to all of you, but knowing that only she can feel how much I'm shaking. Not because I'm scared of this journey but because I *never* want to fail her."

There is nothing like love – Nothing like real love. I must have stared into his bluish green eyes all night because I felt secure in us. I was promised a life of joy, security, and adoration for one small price; be the perfect wife. I cried every time I thought of that moment. Not only did he adore the ground I walked on, but he also made sure to show me at every turn. We trusted each other but most importantly, we *knew* each other.

As a wife, I prided myself on being J.J.'s everything, not just in household duties but in being his friend, lover, business partner and confidant. We never had problems in the communication department or even in the bedroom and rarely had big arguments. For the most part, I got what I wanted, when I wanted it. We mutually respected and gave each other space to be who we were, and to do what we do personally and professionally. It was odd to most people that we were so brutally honest with each other, but it worked for us.

As for James' career, he was among the who's who of corporate attorneys. He and I enjoyed the benefit of camaraderie among his colleagues to a greater degree than most. It takes lots of stamina, a sharp mind, and excellent communication skills for a corporate lawyer to build the kind of reputation that J.J. has built. So privacy was always a big deal between us.

I walked into a hurricane one night

about nine months ago when I pulled into my driveway and noticed there was a strange car in my parking space. I shrugged it off because my popular stud of a husband frequently entertained his friends and their "other" women at our home. You know; *the side-chick*.' The type of female that knows the guy she is messing around with has a wife or 'main-chick.' We always fought about this because not only was I friends with some of their wives, I respected these same men. I was always stuck between a rock and a hard place. My favorite aunt Juanita always said, "Stay out of grown folks business. Nobody wants to think of themselves as someone who's being played." I used to think I'd react differently, but when there's a lot invested in a relationship, it's sometimes easier to blame the person who's smashing your rose-tinted glasses than the one who's breaking your heart.

I started thinking about whether I'd want to hear news like that from a friend. There were so many things to consider which always led to the "shoot the messenger" reaction. As my mind trailed, the soft spot in my heart started to swell. I couldn't help asking all the questions I am sure so many other women ask. *Do you believe your friend? Do you believe your husband or your wife? Do you want to hear their advice after they tell you what they saw? Do you want to break up a marriage? Do you want to break up a family? Can you – should you work through the issues in your marriage? Would God punish you for leaving? I mean, even Jesus forgave the woman at the well.*

The thought was so sobering I quickly snapped back to reality. "My aunt is right. We should stay out of other people's relationships simply because it's the way God intended." I shook it off with my Pastor's little reminder, "Let marriage be held in honor among all, and let the marriage bed be undefiled, for God will judge the sexually immoral and adulterous." *How funny*, I thought, *I'm not normally this spiritual about things.*

My heart melted as I sat inside my brand new birthday gift – a fully loaded bronze BMW X5 SUV including heated seats and a moonroof to die for – and thought about how much my husband and I loved each other. A smile crept its way onto my face and I grabbed my clear coconut flavored lip gloss out of the front pocket of my black and red soft leather handbag and swiped it across the full lips I was blessed with, rubbed them together making a 'popping' sound, and quickly exited the vehicle. I bounded up the stairs to the front door hearing the faint sound of music in the air.

Wait, I paused, That's Maxwell's "Don't Ever Wonder", *Why is that playing?* The locked clicked and the door squeaked as I swung the large wooden oak door open. I stopped and heard some commotion in my kitchen. I walked toward the kitchen door calling J.J.'s name, no answer. As I entered the kitchen, the back door was wide open and a breathless J.J. stumbled through the screen door.

"Oh! *Hey, babe!*" J.J. squealed.

"Hey," I said suspiciously.

"How was your day?" He asked moving toward the sink.

"My day was fine. How was yours."

"Way too busy for words," He said as he rinsed his mouth with the faucet water.

"You ok?" I questioned.

"Yeah. Why?"

"What's wrong with your mouth?"

"Nothing. Just a funny taste." James did not turn around.

"Whose car is that?"

"What car?"

"The one in the driveway James!"

"Oh...that car." He squeaked again. "Don't be mad – "

"Mad about what!" I barked back.

"That was Wesley's girl. She stopped by to see if I could read something for her."

"So where is she?"

"He came by to pick her up. They were arguing about something. I told him to leave the car here and go take care of their business." He quickly replied.

"So what were you doing outside?"

"I was taking out the trash." He and I looked over at the trash can near the door.

"Um, James..." I said peering back at him pointing to the still full trash can next to the door.

"I took the trash from the bathrooms upstairs out. Now I'm going to take this one when we are done with dinner." I looked at him with a side eye and he glided past me. "By the way, what's for dinner anyway?" He said as he kissed me on the cheek and walked into the living room.

I followed behind him still not convinced of his story, "What do you take me for, a fool?"

"No babe." He stopped and turned around. "You know Wesley got hoes for days! This is one of the new ones and she is getting divorced and he told her that I would look over some papers. I didn't even know she was coming by until she showed up." J.J. explained.

"*Right.* Next you're going to tell me that the Easter Bunny exists!"

His cheeks formed a smirk as he put his arms around my waist. "I only have eyes for you. I already told Wes that he can't do that anymore. He might be trying to have me killed. He knows you don't play that."

"James Jones Taylor," I smiled. "I will kill you until you die if I ever catch another woman in my house without me being here."

"I know. I'm sorry."

"You better be sure she rings this bell when she comes back for that car."

"Yes, dear. Are you ready for your girls' trip?" He changed the subject.

"I'm packed if that's what you mean." I walked past him toward the stairs.

"You know you're going to miss me when you're gone."

"Let you tell it!" I laughed. "Tina and I

are going out so don't expect me home for dinner."

"I never do when the two of you get together." He shook his head.

I reached the top of the stairs and went directly into the bathroom where I immediately

looked at the trash can. It wasn't empty. My jaw tightened. In that instant my life literally changed – like a ripple effect in space & time – I felt it. If I hadn't stayed awake and heard that woman myself, I never would have believed it. When I realized J.J. was lying to me about who had been in our home, I wanted to die. But instead, I pretended to fall asleep on the couch. That's when I heard him open the back door. There he was, in our driveway hugging a woman who I couldn't completely see out in the darkness and telling her not to come here again. She apologized and leaned in to kiss *my husband*. James turned his head and landed in my direction. He shoved the woman in her car as I came running toward them. "So this is what you were doing? Who is that James?" I yelled at the mystery woman who backed out of our driveway and onto the street in one swift motion.

"It's not what you think babe!"

"You are kissing some hoe in my driveway and telling her not to come back and it's not what *I* think! That's the best you can do James!" I screamed in his face.

"Calm down. Let me explain."

"No! I gave you that chance and you lied

to my face!"

"Babe. Listen to me. I didn't –" I muffed his face before he could finish the sentence. I was so furious I hadn't realized he'd picked me up and was carrying me back into the house. "Calm down. Someone is going to call the police!"

"They should! You better hope they do because I'm gonna kill you!" I said wildly swinging my arms and legs. I wasn't going to land any real punches that way so I did the next best thing – I started throwing anything I could get my hands on. It didn't matter what it was, I threw it. James dodged a few and I landed a few. When I grew tired, I packed his clothes and threw them out the front door. "Get the hell out! NOW!" I demanded.

"When you calm down, call me!" He said grabbing his keys from the drawer in the foyer.

"The only calm you will get from me is when I'm dancing on your grave!" I blurted out. I must admit, even that statement surprised me, but I said it so I had to stand by it. I locked the door behind him and went upstairs.

The next thing I knew I was awakened by the sound of my alarm clock playing my favorite radio personality, Johnny "Koolout" Starks, reciting his trademarked slogan, *"When life puts too much on your plate, don't stress – Koolout!"* I slowly peeled back the covers and gingerly moved my body to the edge of the bed. Every inch of me hurt, it felt like I'd been hit by a truck. With one deep breath that nearly crushed my lungs when I exhaled, my feet hit the floor. *Thank GOD for small miracles*.

I looked around the oversized coral painted room. For the first time I noticed the windows had no dressing, just a simple white blind covering them. I stood perfectly still, marveling at the feeling of strength and trying to make a move. *Why did I pick this color?* I asked. *Because it was bright and warm...that's right!* I answered. I glanced to the right a noticed the cream nightstand that stood as tall as my bed. It was a handcrafted antique, simple in design, with one door and one drawer. The perfect fit for my heat censored lamp and small clock radio alarm.

I remembered how bad I'd wanted that single night stand and how I'd admired it for weeks in the store. It coordinated perfectly with my antique oak dresser and armoire. My attention was drawn across the room to the single picture hanging on the wall – I almost lost my footing. There we were happily holding hands in our wedding photo. I felt a rush of heat over my entire body and my legs trembled. *Why did he do this? What have I done!* My body writhed in pain. I wanted my life back. I wanted to be normal again. I don't want excitement or lies or lust. I wanted routine, romance, and arguments over how to fold the towels, normalcy, and the same old "what do you want for dinner" conversation that drove me nuts. *What happened?* I looked around at my beautiful, specially selected things, they felt so sad. All these things that were so important meant nothing anymore.

The massacre of the room registered slowly as I inched my way toward the edge of the bed, the feeling of the physical pain to return to my consciousness. The confusion of why my body hurt so fiercely quickly subsided when I noticed all the bright and dark bruising on my left arm and right leg. "Ouch! What the fuck was that?!" I looked down at the blood oozing down my ankle and onto the hardwood floor making a slippery puddle beneath me. The jagged edge of the broken glass from the wine bottle I'd thrown at J.J.'s head had rolled partly underneath the bed and come back to remind me of the near death fight that had taken place in my once happy home. *Bastard!* I couldn't believe my life was turning to shit right in front of me. If this was God's sense of humor, it was morbid in every way!

My adoring hubby's love turned into a heated hatred that I've never had the pleasure of encountering in the years I'd known him. Oh! The cat was out the bag! The handsome and successful Mr. James Jones Taylor, decided I wasn't enough of a wife for him anymore, my body wasn't what he wanted and my lofty ambitions were never practical enough to deserve his support. I'm sure some things were said out of anger and others were true, which was what I didn't know.

SIMPLE

6:00 A.M. the following Friday, rather than having J.J. take me to the airport as I usually do, I called a cab and waited at the curb with three pieces of luggage and my laptop. I needed to be comfortable so I put on my favorite extra long black yoga pants, fitted red and black baby tee with my trademarked business slogan, "Cheers to New Careers" splashed across the front of a martini glass, and all white classic K-Swiss gym shoes. When the taxi arrived, I didn't even wait for the driver to help me with my bags. I tossed them into the back seat, slid into the only open area left, slammed the door, folded my arms across my chest and said, "Airport! Step on it!" Without saying a word, the driver looked at me puzzled, pressed the meter and pulled away from my broken home.

After a long and silent twenty minute drive I pulled a fifty dollar bill from my bag, thanked the driver, and exited the vehicle. "Wait. Miss...your change." He said as I jumped out of the passenger side.

"Keep it," I said flatly. "Thanks for not talking, this might not have been so pleasant if you had." I continued as I yanked my bags from the back seat. The driver looked puzzled and cautiously closed the doors that I'd carelessly left open. I took a moment and attached each red leather bag to the other and started toward to automatic doors of the airport, I swore I heard someone calling my name. "Desi! Desiree!" I stopped, looked around but didn't see anyone that I could immediately identify, so I continued my enraged walk toward the counter.

Good no line, I thought as I approached the ticket agent.

"Good morning. Where are you flying today?" The annoyingly perky ticket agent squeaked.

"Far away from here!" I snapped back.

"Oh! That can be a good thing. And from the look of it I hope it's the best destination to change your mood." She responded with effortless sarcasm. My eyes darted at the agent with a look that clearly said *'You can always be my next victim.'* But before I could reply with my snide comment she added, "May I have your ID, please." I fumbled around in my small red leather carry-on bag with my initials, *D.E.T.*, elegantly etched into each side until I found my identification, "Here."

"Thank you," She said with a fake smile taking my license from my hand. "That's a *really* nice ring," She added staring at the oversized three leveled diamond resting on my finger. I froze momentarily to process the ring and what she'd just said. Once again, before I could reply she interjected another compliment. "I *love* your bag as well! You have great taste. I've never seen anything like that before – definitely unique! Is that the name of the designer?" She pointed to the side etching.

"No –" I softened, "They're my initials. The bag was handmade special for me, a gift from my husband." I gave a half-hearted smile. "But the letters have a double meaning; *Don't Even Think* about it." Surprised by my intentionally snarky detailed answer, she slid my printed ticket across the counter while another attendant placed my checked bags on the conveyor belt.

"Gate C35. Your flight is delayed. Have a great time." I snatched the ticket and strutted my way to the security checkpoint slightly embarrassed at how I'd just treated that poor unsuspecting woman. I thought about going back to apologize when I felt a tap on my shoulder.

"Hey!"

"Oh my gosh, hello!" I stopped strutting and gave the pleasantly surprised acquaintance a big hug.

"You are a hard woman to catch up with," Raymond said catching his breath.

"What do you mean?"

"I saw you when you arrived. I was calling your name, but I guess you didn't hear me."

"Oh! That was you?" I blushed. "Where are you off to?" I quickly recovered.

"Ah, here and there....You know."

"I see," I said with a huge smile. Raymond was a site to behold, always a gentlemen. I took a brief moment to drink him. "Catch your breath silly.

You chased me and now you've caught me." My eyes scanned every inch of his five foot, eleven-inch muscular caramel skinned frame. I wasn't sure if it was his hazel eyes, curly black hair, smooth skin, well-manicured hands and beard – you know, the thin line trace from ear to ear – round cheeks or slightly deep baritone voice that got my panties wet every time we saw each other, but on this day I didn't want to figure it out. I just went with it, I didn't care if it showed or not, but I guess it did. Before I could regain my composure, he leaned in to catch me with another hug. He smelled of Jean Paul Gaultier cologne. I loved that fragrance! I bought it often enough for James. As I inhaled him, I heard the sound of him breathing in the scent of my hair, followed by the pulse of his penis pulse. This hug was a game changer. *How could he know that I needed that hug? How could he be here, right now, at this exact moment? How was it that this man had all the perfect timing in the world?* I could tell we'd held each other a little too long because we were startled when the woman from the counter interrupted us.

"Excuse me, Mrs. Taylor!" We jumped and separated. "You took your ticket but left your ID."

"Thank you. You're too kind." I smiled like I'd been caught with my hand in the cookie jar.

"This *must* be Mr. Taylor, the lucky man with the impeccable taste in jewelry and luggage." Raymond and I looked at the nosey attendant then back at each other and laughed.

"Yes!" He looked at me. "Yes, I *must* be

26

Mr. Taylor, the man with the impeccable taste in jewelry and luggage." He laughed harder as he reached for the handle of my carry-on bag and took my hand. We turned and walked toward the security check glancing and giggling at each other.

I had two full hours to fill before my flight departed and I knew Tina wouldn't arrive until the absolute last minute. Even then she'd probably need the captain to hold the plane. We walked slow, stopped for a scone and chit chatted about the weather, business, his latest girlfriend, and my marriage. Ray hung on my every word and me on his. See, things with Raymond were always relaxed and simple. We'd met during a business meeting a few years back, he consulted on a construction project for a client we shared. I complimented him on the use of Brownstone and Victorian architecture in his recommendations. We instantly connected on an intellectual level and it didn't hurt that we were attractive individuals.

"So enlighten me about your husband." He eagerly asked.

"It was simple. Now it's not." I answered shamefully.

"So you like simple?"

"Don't you?" I came back.

"Yes. Yes, I do." He emphatically.

"How do you stay so…simple?" I inquired.

"Easy. I just keep it simple." We burst with laughter and he continued with an explanation. "Simple to me is going with what feels right and enjoying the moment. For example, it would be simple for me to take you into *that* family bathroom and lick your inner thighs until I land on the little almond in the center and tickle it with my tongue until you beg me to stop. That would be simple, plus I'd enjoy every minute."

I swallowed my orange juice hard and tried not to choke as I stared him in the eyes. Every ounce of me believed he could feel my wetness from across the table. He confirmed when he placed his large hands on my thigh and started to rub.

"You would die if I said yes," I said in an attempt to level the playing field.

"You will never know until you say it." He locked his eyes with mine and challenged me.

"Yes." I didn't care or at least I didn't want to. I stood, grabbed my bag and walked across the lounge area to the family bathroom without looking back. I blocked out all traces of J.J. and decided I wasn't going to allow personal points for good behavior. *Why?* All the faithful years didn't matter anyway, they meant nothing to him, and so they shouldn't mean anything to me. I heard the door close and lock behind me.

Raymond dropped his bag and placed his hands on my face, forcing his tongue into my mouth. I dropped my bag too. We shared an equally deep and passionate kiss. He pulled down my pants and underwear in one move and placed me on the counter. This was dirty and I loved it! It was not what a good girl, or wife for that matter, would or even should do. It was all wrong and I wanted it. *Fuck J.J.! He can have that other chick! She was bold enough to come into my house and he was dumb enough to let her!* I rationalized. And wasn't going to ever fuck Raymond...just allow him to air my orchid, get on my flight, and start my vacation off right!

My vagina throbbed with anticipation. Ray knelt before me, forced my legs apart, and didn't waste a nanosecond going in. He didn't bother tracing any part of my thigh as promised. He pointed his tongue like a dart and flicked the center of my cherry, my full head of feathered hair fell back, and I moaned in a low voice.

"Nope," He said.

"Wh-at?"

"Nope." He moved his mouth back long enough to instruct me. "No holding back. I want to hear you."

"Ok," I whispered. He plunged his face between my thighs and sucked and licked it in circles.

"Oh- my-gosh!" I squealed.

"Nope." He continued to slurp.

"*Ahhh*" I moaned louder.

"Nope." He sucked harder.

My hands gripped his shoulders and I noticed how my wedding ring sparkled under the fluorescent lights of the bathroom. "YES! YES! OH –MY-GOD! YES!" I came hard. He lifted himself from between my thighs with my creamy juices plastered over his face.

"Do you know how long I've waited to do that...again?"

"No," I said shaking my head with a smirk.

"Since the day we met. I always seem to have great timing." He said standing. I sat up straight then jumped down from the counter and reached for my pants.

"Thank you," I said politely, stepping into my underwear.

"You're welcome. The pleasure was all mine." With a gigantic smile, he assisted in pulling up my yoga pants. I wet a paper towel and wiped my excitement from his face.

I broke the silence first. "I'm walking out first."

"Be my guest." He laughed deep.

I quickly picked up my bag, tossed the moist paper towel in the open trash can, adjusted my clothes along with hair and walked out of the bathroom. I couldn't decide if I was happier at what had taken place or at the looks on the faces of the people sitting in earshot of my marital crime scene. *Who cares! My gate was on the other side of the airport anyway. I don't have to board a flight with these looky-loos.* "Don't judge me," I said as I laughed out loud. Seconds later Raymond followed. He grabbed my hand when he caught up to me. I accepted for a few seconds then released it, he looked at me confused.

"Simple," I said. "I've got to get to my gate. By the way, where is yours?"

"It's on the way."

"Well, give me my hug now. Until next time my friend." I said pausing for the hug. He obliged and we continued the stroll. We arrived at C35 and there sat my best friend, Tina, reading a magazine. I shot Raymond a *play it cool* look and he nodded.

"Hey, Tina!" I said snatching the magazine.

"Hey, girl! Are you ready?" She said excitedly.

"Oh yeah! I'm definitely ready!" I looked at Ray.

"And *who* is this?" She questioned as she inserted herself between Raymond and me.

"Well excuse me! Dang! Tina, this is a colleague of mine, Raymond Humphrey. Raymond, this is my best friend, Tina Harper."

"Look at that! If we got married, I wouldn't have to change my initials." She laughed at her own joke.

"Um…okay. Nice to meet you, Ms.Tina Harper." Ray extended his hand.

"And a gentlemen too!" She extended her hand.

"So! I see you ladies are off for a little fun in the sun in Tampa."

"Yes, St. Petersburg to be exact," Tina informed him.

"Oh really!" He nodded looking at me.

"Flight 0929 now boarding." The gate attendant announced.

"Well, that's us!" I said in a sudden desperate attempt to break up the conversation.

"Where are the friendly skies delivering you Mr. Humphrey?"

"Looks like we're on the same flight." He looked at me, then back to Tina. "We will have plenty of time to catch up on the plane." My heart pounded in my chest so hard I thought Tina could surely see it – she didn't. She was too busy flirting with the man I'd just had a head affair within the concourse bathroom. Tina inserted her arm around Ray's and commented on his muscles as I trailed behind them all of a sudden wishing I had resisted my 'bad girl' moment.

The flight took off and landed without incident. As we exited the plane, Ray helped us with our bags and we chit chatted our way to the baggage claim. I was amazed at how easy it was for Ray to act nonchalant about what had taken place. We retrieved our luggage from the carousel and went to the rental car counter where Ray jotted down his hotel information and cell phone number. I was amused at our choice of convertibles rentals and bid him goodbye.

"Are the other girls here already?" Tina asked.

"I think so. If not they are not too far behind." We all came in on different flights, two by two, from our respective parts of the world.

GOD TOOK A HOLIDAY
AND SO DID I

Tina, the best friend a person could ever have. You know that friend that you tell your deepest darkest secrets to – yeah that's her! We're our own reality show and sitcom; The Golden Girls theme song plays whenever we're together. My friend was physically one of the most beautiful women the world has ever seen, but she tended to be a really ugly person on the inside. I was the only real female friend she had; other women only tolerated her because of me. I didn't mind because I knew I could be myself around her and she was always brutally honest with me. She didn't treat me like I always had the answers, we balanced each other.

While we awaited the arrival of the rest of our female entourage; Sasha, Tara, Angel, Trisha, and Kim, we took lunch at our favorite spot, the nail salon. We found two open massive leather massaging chairs and the hostess handed us each a bottle of water and asked, "Would you like anything else?" We responded with a simultaneous, "No thank you." immediately followed by, "Jinx!"

"So what have you been up to?" Tina asked eagerly.

"Nothing much....Just trying to move to the next level." I quipped.

"What next level?"

"You know life, work, and stuff like that," I said with a serious face. "Actually…there is something I want – no, need to talk to you about.

"*Ooh!* This sounds juicy! You just got way too serious girl!"

"It is. Or at least I think it is."

"Stop beating around the bush and dish," Tina said giving me her full attention.

"Well, okay, I'm bored – in my marriage. And I think J.J. has eyes for another woman." I confessed.

"Hush girl! You know that's not true!" She thought for a second. "But why do you think that?" Tina slapped my arm.

"Because when I came home the other night there was a car in my driveway, I heard that Maxwell song playing *really* loud and when I came into the house he was coming through the back door and jumped when I said, "Hi." I could have *sworn* I heard a female voice. He got all defensive and started lying about taking out the trash and Wesley. Before I went to bed I – "

"Girl stop it! Did you ask him?"

"*Hell yeah,* I asked him! He basically called me delusional and we *both* know that the furthest thing from the truth.

"Lying ass men! That's why I stay single. Can't trust them as far as I can throw 'em. So what are you gonna do now? Oh, I know, stake out!"

"No! Not my style." I shook my head.

"Okay, honestly sweetheart, if that's all you have to go on maybe it's not what you think."

"Maybe." I lied. There was no need to tell her about the woman, I'd just look foolish.

"You did say you were bored. Your mind might be playing tricks on you to spark up a little excitement."

"Okay, *now* who sounds delusional Tina, me or you?" I laughed.

"I'm bored because he doesn't pay attention to me. He doesn't give me the time of day. Our sex life is nothing and he spends more time with those loser friends of his and their side chicks – I think they may be rubbing off on him." I explained.

"Do you think he knows?" She asked.

"Knows about what?" I glanced at her over my bottle of water.

"You know!"

"Of course not! And that doesn't count anyway."

"Why? 'Cause eating ain't cheatin'!" She laughed.

"You're a jerk! And I love you for it." I chuckled.

"Aw hell, what are friends for! It's my job to give you a hard time?"

"HA! There are some things in life you just

don't need to experience. But that man's tongue isn't one of them!"

"Girl are you ever gonna tell me who this mystery man is? "

"Nope." I chuckled at my mocking of Ray in the airport bathroom.

"Okay. Fine. Be like that."

"Okay. No problem." The sudden seriousness of my voice wiped the smile from her face.

"Oh! So it's like that, huh!"

"I've shared enough already. You don't need to know all the players involved in this game."

"Game."

"Yes, game," I repeated. "That's how I look at it. It keeps things interesting and strategic, like a business."

"This is *not* business Desi. This is real life and you are going to ruin your perfect little life and end up heartbroken in the end."

"I appreciate your concern, but I've thought about all the possible endings."

"*Hmmm.* I'm not sure you have considered *all* the possible endings, Desi."

"I'm a realist Tina! Playing this *game* means sacrificing your own heart as a casualty. I am willing to bet on myself. Besides, a girl is allowed to have a little fun, every now and again."

"Not the kind of fun that will fuck you in the end....And not in a good way."

"Since when did you become the voice of reason?"

"Since I met the man of my dreams in the

airport. I've seen him before but damn! I think this is a sign. He is the kinda man I can see myself with. *Mmmm. Mmmm.* Delicious."

I choked on the water I was trying to swallow. Tina was too caught in her own fantasy to notice and continued without interruption. "I bet he could put it down too! I got wet just thinking about his voice. *Girl*, that voice could melt the panties off any woman. I think I'm going to have to bump into him while we're here at least once, twice, maybe three times."

"Um…earth to Tina." I snapped my fingers to get her attention.

"What girl! Don't interrupt me! I was almost there!"

"I think he might be involved."

"*With who?* I didn't see a ring."

"Not married, involved. *You know*, involved. Plus, I hear he's a playboy."

"So! So am I. I just want to taste it." Tina teased.

"Never play that close to home."

"I'm not. I'm on vacation and so his he." She raised her hand for a high five.

"Yeah, you're right. Go for it." I swallowed hard. I know Ray was an expert at keeping secrets, but I didn't want him to take my best friend up on *any* offers. I high-fived my friend and said a prayer to whatever god was listening. My cell phone rang, it was Sasha. The rest of the girls had just arrived and were waiting for us at the condo. "Let the fun begin! The girls are here and we are fabulous!" Florida was always my favorite place in the world, any part of the state suited me just fine. With that declaration, Desiree took a backseat and Desi was in control.

FORGIVENESS VS. PERMISSION

Back at the hotel we pulled out our best get-'em-girl dresses and prepared for the night ahead. I decided to put on a little red number with spaghetti straps and crinkled center. My five-inch silver Guess heels were the perfect complement to my silver jewelry and clutch. My hair had the perfect bounce and swayed when I walked. And my cleavage was propped up enough to draw attention but not enough for a Janet Jackson moment on the dance floor. Our vacation ritual of the night was to shut off our cell phones and powered up our alternates. I added Ray's number to my temporary contact list, just in case. This way anyone we dated, married, or called a significant other couldn't say they were able to reach one of us while trying to contact his intended. I loved exploring what and who Florida had to offer. I'm a huge flirt, but it never went anywhere, I mean, come on, I'm married not dead!

We synchronized our alternates with each other's phone number and performed a test call and text to be sure everything was in working order. I must admit I enjoyed these covert operations a little too much. They made me feel alive, sexy, and most of all dangerous!

"What are you doing?" Sasha asked peeking into my bedroom.

I jumped and fumbled my phone. "Nothing."

"Are you breaking the rules Desi?"

"No! Of course not!" I laughed nervously.

"So what are you doing?" Sasha charged toward the bed where I was sitting.

"Just adding an extra insurance policy to my trip, that's all," I smirked.

"*Insurance policy?*" Sasha repeated.

I stood to protect my screen. "Yep!" I pushed past her and smiled.

"Hey ya'll! Desi is up to something!" Sasha ran into the living room tattling like a child.

"Oh my gosh! What are you talking about?! I'm not up to anything, *damn*! Mind your own business." I laughed hard. "I'm ready to go and do what I do best! So if you hags want to sit around here any longer, the next sound you will hear will be my wheels screeching from the parking lot! Last one to Storman's buys three rounds!" I took my keys and strutted down the hallway of our condo letting the door slam behind me. Like clockwork, the entourage followed. We piled into our respective convertibles and peeled away from the parking lot as if we had no concept what a brake pedal was meant for.

A short time later we arrived at our first stop, Storman's night club. The valet waved us forward toward where three of the most handsome men opened each of our car doors. My valet was tall and Cuban, Sasha's was black and well built, and Trisha's was a very exotic looking white man with a perfect pair of hazel eyes. Each helped us with the offering of a hand, I tipped in advance just for that!

"Nice legs!" He said in a low voice.

"Thank you," I responded with a wink.

"Top up or down?"

"Player's choice," I said leaning to adjust my diamond heart ankle bracelet. The cars roared into the first three spaces in front of the club. You could feel the beat of the music thumping throughout the thick, white walls of the building.

"I guess we make this place look good," Trisha said pointing to the growing crowd of spectators trying to figure out who we were.

"I guess so!" Angel giggled.

"Tonight no one holds back!" Tara pointed at Sasha.

"Let's dance!" Sasha smacked her accusing finger away.

As we approached the entrance, the security acknowledged us with a smile then removed the velvet rope without asking for ID. No cover. No ID check. No questions. A female hostess approached us and led us to an elevated seating area with a view of the club. *I know we're always star status, but this was strange even for me.*

"Can I get you anything?"

"Give us a few minutes." Tara politely asked.

"Ok ladies! Which of you phoned ahead? And whoever it was, THANK YOU! I feel like a celebrity!" Angel wiggled.

"It wasn't me." Tara chimed.

"Not me," Trisha said sat back against the leather couch.

"Me either!" Tina pointed.

"So that's what you were doing Desi!" Sasha shouted.

"Nope. I wish I could take credit for this one, but I can't. The next spot, *that's* a different story!"

"Don't look a gift horse in the mouth! Let's just see where this goes." Sasha rolled her neck. I shrugged my shoulders and waived the sexy little hostess over. I ordered a round of shots, two bottles of Hennessey Black, and a bottle of apple juice. We danced and checked out the scenery. The young lady returned with all that I'd requested including a bottle of Top Brass Vodka with a pitcher of cranberry juice.

"Oh, I'm sorry miss – what's your name?"

"Stephanie."

"Sorry Steph, we didn't order this." I pointed to the other items.

"No, you didn't." She giggled. "But *he* insisted that you have it." She pointed across the club.

"Oh really!" The smile on my face spread. "That man is too much sometimes."

"Should I put it down?"

"Yes. Please."

"Let me know if there is anything I can do for

you," Stephanie added.

"Wait! There is one thing." I scribbled on a napkin, folded it and handed it to her. "Can you give this to the handsome gentlemen that sent the drinks?" As she took the napkin from my hands, I admired her frame. She was well put together or maintained; whichever happened to be the case. Stephanie's waist was trim and her hips were wide, her breasts seemed to say, *Is it me or is it cold in here?* As I watched my friends dance and laugh I couldn't help but think I've always had and admiration for the human body, male or female. If you've got a great ass, you've got a great ass. If you've got a great chest, you've got a great chest. I was never big on comparisons either. I liked the thickness of my curves. I appreciated them. When it came to appearances, none of my friends had flaws in my eyes, they were all different. I drew my attention away from the physical attributes of my female girl crew and searched the club for Raymond. My eyes couldn't find him anywhere.

"Looking for someone?" He tapped me on the shoulder.

I jumped. "Boy! Don't scare me like that!"

He kissed my check, "Didn't mean to startle you. I just wanted to deliver my comment to this lovely note in person.

"*Oh.*" I crossed my legs on the white leather couch and twisted them in his direction. He poured the vodka and cranberry into a glass, added ice and handed it to me.

"Simple," He said with a grin.

"That's what I wrote, isn't it."

"Yes. And *that* is what I'm saying to you. Just like your favorite drink, simple." His subtle assertiveness turned me on. For a moment, I was afraid to move for fear there would be a wet spot underneath me.

"You call this simple?" I asked coyly.

"You've got your definition and I've got mine."

"How did you even know I would be here?"

"Your friend slipped me a note with your whole itinerary on the plane."

"Oh my God, Tina!" Tina turned around.

"Look who's here ladies!" Tina said.

"And who is this handsome fellow?" Sasha extended her hand.

"My name is Raymond, but my friends call me Ray." He kissed Sasha's hand.

"Nice to meet you, Ray." Sasha blushed.

"Ray, this is Tara, Angel, Trisha, Sasha, and you've already met Tina."

"So you're who we need to thank for this," Angel said with a Vana White showcase wave.

Ray slightly shrugged, "No need to thank me. I'm just glad I could be a good host."

"Good host is an understatement!" Tina wiggled her way into the small space between Ray and me.

"*Smooth,*" I whispered in Tina's ear.

Tina ignored me and continued with her desperate crack at attention, "So how much is something like this costing you Ray?"

"Girl stop trying to count that man's money!" Trisha pulled Tina.

Tina snatched her arm away from Trisha. "I'm not! I'm just asking a question!"

"Ray, please excuse our friend," Trisha said looking at him. "Sometimes she can be so inappropriate." She darted a look at Tina.

"So how do you know our Desiree?" Angel shrieked breaking the awkwardness of the moment.

"Business," Ray answered matter-of-factly.

"Oh, so you're here for business or pleasure?" Sasha asked.

"Both….If I get my way." Ray took a drink.

"I see! I won't get into all that but, thanks! This was a really nice gesture!" Tara said patting his shoulder.

"You're very welcome!" He stood. "Now if you ladies don't mind, I've got to get back to my guests."

"Nice meeting you."

"D, if I don't get to see you again on this trip don't be a stranger." Ray looked me squarely in the eyes. I could tell from his tone of voice, he was going to 'bump' into me again before I left the state.

"I won't." I grinned again. "Thanks again." I stood, adjusted my dress, and gave him a hug. My pussy pulsated and his member throbbed against my thigh. I'd never seen it before, but I'm sure it was impressive. Tina grabbed my hand, breaking my fantasy before it could get started, "Let's go, girl! This is my song!"

Down to the dance floor we went. For the next eight songs, we gyrated into a sweat then returned to our coveted VIP area. I looked into my purse for a tissue and noticed I had four text messages. They could only be from one person because this was my alternate phone and all my friends were on the dance floor with me.

Message #1: *You look incredible! I want to lick every inch of you.*

Message #2: *I see you on the dance floor. I can't concentrate. If you can move like that, I'm scared of what you're like in the bedroom.*

Message #3: *My dick is hard as hell right now! Meet me in the back. Tell Stephanie to show you where it is. I told her to give you access to the office. I'll move when you move.*

Message #4: *This can't get any simpler. ;-)*

Right away I stood and motioned for Stephanie, who glided to my aide. "The office."

"This way." I followed her down the stairs and around a corner to a black door. She unlocked it, said, "Go in." and walked away. I stepped inside the room and closed the door behind me, *what am I thinking?* I answered with a firm, *I'm on vacation from life.* I set my purse on a chair in front of the desk then looked around the room. I hopped on the marble desk then pushed back far enough for my legs to dangle where I crossed them at the knee. No sooner had I straightened my back, the door opened. My heart beat a mile a minute, but I managed to keep my cool.

Ray closed the door slowly. I could tell by the bulge in his pants, his text messages were no lie. From where I sat, I admired him from head to toe, and *damn* this man was a fine specimen! "Why are you over there?"

"Because you didn't ask me to come closer."

His voice was seductive.

"Come. Closer." I beckoned him with my index finger. He looked intently at me, placed his hands in his pockets and walked purposefully toward me, then stopped. "What?"

"I was just thinking how great your lips would look wrapped around my dick."

"My! My! Aren't we forward tonight."

"Should I play it cool?"

"No. Not at all. I don't like bullshit."

"Then put it in your mouth," He said almost unsure if I would accept the challenge.

I stepped off the desk and stood in front of him, "You've got to do something for me first."

"What would that be?"

I took his tie and wrapped it around my hand pulling his face closer to mine. "Get on your knees and ask me nicely." Ray did as I demanded.

"*Please. Please. Please* put Ray in your mouth." I released his tie. Without a sound, I knelt as he stood. We unraveled his belt buckle, button, and zipper. I yanked his pants and briefs down. I was intimidated by what was presented in front of me. Ray was an *easy* 8 to 8.5 inches. His package was thick, long and erect. I placed one hand over the shaft and added the other on top of it, pointed my tongue and flicked the head just enough to taste him. "Don't play with it." He murmured. I opened my mouth wide and extended my neck so I could shove it all in at once until the head touched the back of my throat. Recognizing that I was a bit of an amateur, he moved his hips as if he were inside me. I chocked on it a few times before I got a good rhythm. My saliva dripped and his moans started exciting me. He placed his hands on my head to control his reaction and the sound of slurping rendered the thong underneath my dress as no good. I removed my hands and raised my dress over my hips while I continued to suck Ray's dick like a straw. For just a split second, I looked at him and we knew it was time, penetration was all we needed to complete this fantasy.

He helped me up from the floor and walked backward to a couch. For a second, I wondered how many asses had gotten laid in this very spot but quickly released the thought. I laid down with my back to the couch and he stood in front of me. I extended my legs just enough for him to know I was ready for whatever, whenever he was. He spread them wider. He pushed my legs apart then up and held them there. "Wait." I stopped him, "Do you have a condom?" With no response, he glided into my pussy with such a force that I screamed. Either he didn't hear me or he didn't care because he didn't stop. It hurt at first, but I quickly realized he wasn't trying to hurt me. I was experiencing a level of ecstasy that didn't have boundaries. He was so deep – I didn't know how to handle it. *Pain that felt good?* Each time he repeated the move he looked for a change in my reaction. He leaned forward with the last thrust and said, "Pain is suggestive. Desiree is a pleasure." I relaxed and came. He adjusted his wood then reached into the pocket of his pants lying on the floor nearby and retrieved a condom. *Now was a good time to remove my thong.* I was relieved at the condom but mad for not stopping him before we started and insisting he put one on. He slid the Magnum XXL over my creamy remnants and entered me again, this time centimeters at a time. When he was all the way inside, his shaft flexed and bounced, it felt like he could lift my entire body with that one limb. I hollered louder than the music thumping on the other side of the walls. My back arched and he pulled my waist into his then scooped me up. I held on for dear life because I was no small girl, but he seemed to handle me with ease. I crossed my legs around his waist and used his shoulders to move. "OH! FUCK ME! PLEASE!"

"Anyway, you want it, babe," He said panting in my ear. Ray placed me back on the couch, this time with my back to the seat cushions. He lifted one leg over his shoulder and leaned into me, only allowing the head of his penis to penetrate me. I bit my bottom lip and our eyes simultaneously rolled.

"I'm going for the kill," He said in a low voice.

"The kill?" I repeated confused.

"Yes!" He spoke softly.

Confused, I pushed back trying to regain control of what was happening but I was too late. He dropped my leg, pulled out and reinserted himself in my behind. He stretched my butt cheeks and went in as deep as my clenched anus would allow. My body went into convulsions. I was mortified! No one had ever done that to me. I mean, I've always wanted to try it, but with J.J. and some lube! *Not like this!* It hurt but felt oddly enjoyable.

Tears ran down my face as I gained the courage to say, "Stop. Please stop."

Ray stopped. He pulled out slow, so as not to

alarm me any further. "Are you ok?"

"I think so."

"I'm so sorry. I just got wrapped up in the moment." He said reaching for my face. I rolled to one side trying to hide tears the tears on my cheeks.

"No. No. I'm fine." I moved gradually toward the edge of the couch. "I've never done that – Let alone *this* before."

"*Oh*....I – "

"Don't say anything," I said sitting up.

"No, Desi, I'm really very sorry."

"I know. I know. It's just, my ass hurts right now." I closed my eyes and breathed through the pain. He tried to read my face because I wouldn't look up at him all the way, but I made eye contact with the falling condom hanging from his steady loss of erection. "Let's not ever mention this again." I finally said looking at him.

"Whatever you say."

"Ray. I've never done this, *EVER!*" I stressed.

"Yeah. I know." He assured me putting on his pants with the condom still attached.

"Um…Ray, you're still connected." I pointed to the condom.

"Oh!" He laughed and grabbed a tissue from the box on the desk. I stood to pull down my dress. Ray picked up my thong and handed it to me, I hid it in my clutch.

"We better get back out there." He teased.

"Yeah, before your girls send out a search party." I looked at my watch and realized we'd been gone for awhile. I reached for the door and Raymond grabbed my hand.

"I'd never do anything to hurt you."

"Never. Speak. Of. This. Again." I said sternly.

"I don't mean it that way." His voice softened.

"What are you talking about then?"

"I mean, I don't just want a fling with you. I'll take it if that's all I can get, but I want you to know that I want more. I can't stop thinking about you."

"The only thing I can concentrate on now is explaining why I'm walking funny." I snickered.

"We'll say you fell and hurt your tailbone, I helped you and you rested in the office."

"You're quick on your feet Mr. Humphrey!"

"Sometimes you have to be!" He joked. We regained our composure then walked backed to the public area of the club where my friends were still sweating on the dance floor. Ray escorted me back to the VIP area. I put on my best sexy walk even though my butt hole was still throbbing with pain. I don't think I accomplished the look that I was going for because Angel came running.

"Oh my gosh, Desi, are you okay?"

"Yes. I'm fine."

"What happened?"

"Nothing. I –"

"She took a pretty hard fall and the staff checked her out in the back." Ray interrupted as my girl clique started to surround me in our VIP haven.

"What in the blue hell!" Tina yelped and pushed Ray from my side. "How the hell did you fall that hard?"

"I'm fine Tina!" I rolled my eyes.

"Ok! Ok! That must've been embarrassing!" Tina chuckled.

"Stop being a jerk Tina!" Sasha hit Tina's arm.

I really just wanted to hide, but I was a grown woman, who did a grown woman thing in the back of a club, no less. I forgot to set rules, so now my only option was to suck it up. I could see Ray out the corner of my eye studying me, again. *God, I wish this man would let me suffer my embarrassment in peace.*

"Thank you, Ray. Please, go check on your other guests. I *really* appreciate the way you've taken care of me – of us." My smile to reassure him that it was okay to leave.

"Okay. I'm going to take my leave." He kissed my cheek.

"*Bye Ray!*" Tina teased as he walked away and turned to me. "So! Did he say anything about me?"

"Nope." I winked.

"Yeah right! Come on, tell me!"

"All I'm going to say is Ray is an interesting person and you ain't ready."

"Girl I stay ready!" She poured a drink. I shook my head at her confidence and giggled because she had no idea the extent of mine and Ray's relationship. She was my best friend, but she didn't know, at least not now. For now, I just wanted to enjoy this time. There is truth to the mystical clarity that comes with going out with your girls when life gets you down, it really does help. Simply enjoying life, laughter, breathing, and relaxation makes all the difference in the world.

Already, I'd forgotten about my fight with my husband. I'd forgotten about how miserable I'd been over the past year. I'd even forgotten about how my ass hurt, for a moment. This life was good. This is the way I'd wanted to feel all the time, minus the aching anus. I wanted my husband to remember me like this, but I didn't think he ever would. So right then and there I made up my mind. *It was better to ask forgiveness than to ask permission.* If I could forgive others then *hell* they could do the same for me. And J.J. needed to know that I wasn't going to stop my life because he found another one and forgot to invite me to the party. I was still furious about the mystery woman in my home and beyond done with the lies and hidden secrecies. I was ready for a divorce. If one of us was going to be unhappy in this marriage, it wasn't going to be me.

"You guys ready to go?" I snapped into reality.

"What time is it?" Trisha asked.

"Five in the morning." Sasha was happy to report.

"What time does this joint close?" Tina asked looking at the crowded club.

"I think six. But I refuse to be in here when the lights come up." I declared.

"Let's go!" We gathered our purses and headed for the door. Stephanie bid us good night with a big smile. The bouncer hustled the valet to retrieve our cars. My ability to walk like a normal person returned. A very handsome gentleman asked my name so I stopped to chat.

"It's Desiree. Like desire." I chided.

"How sexy." He complimented.

"Thank my mother."

"If I ever meet her, I will." He winked and

handed placed a business card in my hand. I looked at it and dropped it in my purse.

"Good night." I beamed. The Florida air was still very warm as the sun came up. Two-by-two, we loaded into our cars and drove back to the condo. All in all, not a bad night. I think I learned something about myself.

TRUTH OR DARE

Over the next four days, I had no contact with Ray. My girls and I performed every girl bonding ritual that make life's moments memorable. We spent countless hours on the beach, snorkeling, parasailing, dinner cruising, banana boating, drinking, shopping, gossiping and of course, our favorite of them all – man watching.

We'd spent the afternoon at a tiki bar on the beach, the sunset and the water was warm. The pink and orange that streaked the sky was picture perfect, so we had the waiter take a snapshot. All six bathing beauties posed in white sarongs, bikinis, or swim suits. Everyone seemed to have divulged the secrets they'd been hiding over the past year. Everyone, accept me. Tina knew a lot about my day-to-day but not every gory detail that excused my over indulgences naughty fantasies. Perhaps I was hosting my own personal sexual revolution. You know the kind that will not be televised. So on our last day in beach heaven I decided to spill my guts.

We took our seats under our cabana complete with fire, red wicker cushioned seating, and sheer drapery. We played truth or dare like a group of teenagers. It was Tara's turn to ask someone a question and I was the lucky target.

"Truth, dare, double dare, or promise to repeat." Tara rattled off.

"*Hmm*...Truth!"

"Who would you sleep with if you had the chance?" Tara fired.

My mood changed the dynamic of the sister circle. I instantly wiped the smile from my face. "So...I've been holding back from you guys. But I really need to say this out loud. It's *really, really,* big. I don't want judgment. I don't need it. I just need to say this." They fell silent.

Trisha put down her fish bowl sized frozen margarita and was the first to speak. "This sounds serious D. Are you sick? Are you pregnant? What is it?"

Not to be outdone, Tina shouted, "Well ya'll

gotta catch up. I know everything already." She picked up her drink and took a sip.

"You know *what*?" Sasha insisted.

"Okay. Well, over the past year James and I have been having a little trouble. I-I mean...we've been arguing a lot and not seeing much of each other. He's made our house into a den for hoes, all in the name of business but I think it's more than that. And before you ask, yes, I've asked him flat out and he says he's not cheating. I don't believe him, especially since he lied to my face." I paused, choking back tears. Angel rubbed my back and I reluctantly continued. "I don't know where or when I went wrong, but he's become a stranger. A few months ago we got in this huge fight over nothing. His phone kept ringing and he was more focused on answering it then finishing the argument." I rambled on. "So...I broke the phone. I was mad and needed him to pay attention to me. He left the house and didn't come back for a week. After the first three days, I tried calling him and fixing the situation but he didn't respond. So I said fuck it. I went to meet a client and someone on the team that I'd been flirting with for awhile made me an offer." All eyes were on me and everyone moved to the edge of their seats in silence and I continued. "I mean seriously! Give me a break! I've been nothing but the perfect wife for so long. I shouldn't have to take this! I wanted to have some fun too damn it!" I started to cry.

"You cheated on James?" Angel gasped.

"Eatin' ain't cheatin'!" Trina interjected.

"Shut up Tina!" Sasha snapped. "This is serious!"

With their mouths wide open, I blurted out the answer to my truth or dare question, "No! Not until I got here!" I cried harder.

"Wait! Wait! What?" Trisha's eyes widened.

"Got here?" Tina spits out her drink. "Here! As in Florida, here?!"

"You heard her!" Tara shouted. "But the only man we saw was the man at the club and-"

"Raymond Humphrey!" Tina hollered.

"You slept with Ray!" Sasha said sitting back.

"When? Where? How?"

I didn't know who was asking which question I just needed to answer them. I took a big gulp of my sangria margarita and wiped my eyes with the cocktail napkin. "Yes. Ray. At the club and the airport. He gave me head and we had sex…anal sex too."

"I don't believe you!"

"Believe it. I don't believe it myself!" I buried my face in my hands.

"*That's* why you were walking funny!" Tina shrieked.

"*Eeew!*" Angel cringed.

"I didn't do it on purpose." I stared at the sand. "We started having regular sex and he slipped it in the back door. I stopped him."

"So the person that ate you before, the one you told me about, that was Ray. The same Ray that met us at the airport, hooked us up in VIP, said you fell and helped you up – that Ray!" Tina clarified.

"YES TINA! YES!" I shouted, ashamed and humiliated.

"*Girrrl!*"

"Were you at least safe?" Trisha took my hand.

"Yes....No...Kinda." I stumbled over my words.

"What do you mean, *kinda*, Desi?" Sasha questioned.

"We started without a condom then he put one on," I recalled.

"This is too deep! I need another drink. Waiter!" Tina called.

"Are you going to tell J.J.?" Trisha asked.

"Hell *no* she's not!" Tina injected again.

"I don't know. I think I want a divorce." I said flatly.

"Divorce!" They replied in unison.

"*Yes!* Divorce. I haven't had sex with my husband in months. *Months!* If he's not doing me, he is doing somebody!"

"Damn!" Angel shook her head.

"I can't do it anymore. I'm not going to live like this. We tore up the house right before I came here. Somebody was in my – *our* house! He lied right to my face! I can't trust him anymore." My tears came hard and fast. "What kind of marriage is that? Huh?"

"He hit you?" Tara questioned me.

"No. We just tussled a bit because I was throwing things at him."

"You know what, if I were you, I'd stay and keep getting yours on the side," Tina instructed. "Yep. Do you. Just like he is. This is why I'm glad I'm single. 'Cause of shit like this."

"What kind of friend gives advice like that?!" Tara got angry.

"A *real* friend! That's what kind. Let's be real, Desiree loves her husband and she is gonna stick it out until there are no options left. So while he has his fun, she should have hers too! Hell, why can't she be satisfied too! I got your back D! You can't be a goodie-goodie your whole life! Welcome to the dark side!" Tina was unyielding.

"Sit down and shut your drunk ass up Tina!" Trisha snapped.

"I'm not drunk! And you shut up!" Tina shouted back.

"Stop it! You guys are causing a scene!" Sasha cautioned.

I got up from my seat. "Yeah, let's drop it. I

need to take a walk, anyway."

"Desi –" Tina started.

"Alone!" I cut her off. I didn't need any more advice. I just wanted the confessional and I got just that. Now it was time to deal with the universe. The ocean was a soothing soundtrack to my stroll. I hadn't noticed that the moon had come out and lit my path along the water into the dark areas of the beach. I continued to cry tears of disgust and confusion. I was mad at myself for being the person I'd always hated. I was disgusted because I acted on crazy impulses and still wanted more. I was actually lusting after another man. I thought about how he'd made it so easy to betray my husband. No one had ever done that before. Believe me, there have been *hundreds* of attempts, including J. J.'s boss. But Ray…Ray had something special, something beyond physicality. He had *'it'*. I got mad all over again, because while I should be trying to figure things out with my husband, I was thinking about Ray. *Focus Desi. Focus.* I shook my head hoping it would shake me back into the right head space. *Now would be a good time to die.* I thought.

Just as I settled into my unavoidable decision to tell my husband that his beloved wife lost his trust, the cell phone resting in my breast beeped. The message read; *Hey there beautiful. I miss you.* Without thinking, I answered, *I miss you too! I was just thinking about you.* Within seconds, he responded. *Meet me tonight for a walk on the beach. Ditch the girls.*

My fingers had a mind of their own, I seized the opportunity. I texted Ray my location and let him know that I was alone. I knew my friends wouldn't come looking for me for a while. Ten minutes later he was walking by my side. I'd forgotten Tina had given him our itinerary. He must have been laying in wait. Oddly enough, most women would have found this creepy but I thought it was sweet how he wanted to be near me. But Ray was smart enough to keep a safe distance until I invited him in. I felt in control over the entire situation. I had to admit Raymond read me so well; he had a special power over me. He had the power to unleash all the suppressed desires of my alter ego. I wanted to act on every impulse I'd ever had with him.

"I don't want to talk," I said almost in a whisper. He didn't speak. We stopped behind a dark rock about three feet tall where he kissed me. I was wearing a two piece tankini swimsuit under my sarong. I don't know when or how but he exposed the massive meat that was his penis and placed my hand around it. I decided the sexier thing to do, was to finish what I'd started in the club a few days earlier. I knelt in the sand and inserted him inside my mouth. He allowed me to suck on the head of his dick for a moment, and then stopped me.

Puzzled, I started to stand but he came down to my level. He placed his hands on my waist and signaled for me to turn around. I obliged. I placed my hand in the water and spread my knees apart wide enough to stabilize myself in the sinking sand. He entered my tunnel with ease just as the ocean water splashed against my arms and washed back out to sea. Ray stroked the walls of my vertical smile steadily. He was so attentive, caring, and smooth. We made no sound and I didn't look back either. I just enjoyed the calm and the massage. This was amazing, I came twice! My body tingled in every place imaginable. I didn't want him to stop. I even imagined him cumming all over the small of my back. I felt a tug on my head and realized he was pulling my hair with just enough force to arch my back and pull my pelvis even closer to his. The rush of feelings, coupled with the waves sent me into a fit. My body said scream but my mouth wouldn't open. He released his grip from my hair and pushed me forward from my butt cheeks. I didn't fall. I turned to confirm what I already knew, he was cumming. He stroked his third leg to direct the flow of sticky liquids streaming from his opening. There was no need to speak, he shook his head and gave me a wide smile.

"I've got to get back," I said as I walked away. By the time I returned to the cabana, Ray messaged me once more:

"*I am a man. You are a woman. I will only let you control this thing for a time. Then...you get the idea. And in case you're wondering...YOUR PUSSY IS THE BEST I'VE EVER HAD!*"

HA! I laughed and thought, *I think I like this.* I sat down as if nothing happened and said, "Whose turn is it? Trisha, truth, dare, double dare or promise to repeat?" My friends thought I was crazy.

CHOICES

On our last night in vacation paradise, we roamed the streets of Ybor City. Ybor was the exotic part of Tampa, also known as Little Chicago – a reference to organized crime, and Ybor City was where it happened. The old brick buildings on 7th Avenue had been converted into bars, restaurants, and nightclubs. Traffic in the area was so jam packed that the city closed 7th Avenue to all traffic and built parking garages. The blocks surrounding 7th Avenue are always buzzing with people. Yes, Ybor City was a party destination!

For one silly reason or another, we wore black dresses and red heels. Although our accessories were varied, we looked uniformly stunning. We sashayed in the first club, ordered frozen drinks and walked the streets looking for the next spot to jump out at us. We stopped at a club reminiscent of the French Quarter, Bourbon Street in New Orleans. We joined the group of club goers in the line when we were approached by a gentleman in a black suit.

He introduced himself as the owner of the establishment and asked where we were from, then motioned the security personnel standing at the VIP entrance.

"Please escort these beautiful ladies to the second floor VIP area. Make sure they get a complimentary bottle of whatever they want." He offered his arm to Sasha. "Ladies."

Tina whispered in my ear, "I think Mr. Humphrey is at it again."

"No," I whispered back.

"You sure?" She chuckled.

"No really, he isn't, this one is on me. The DJ and manager are good friends of mine. I'm trying to get Sasha a husband." Trisha laughed behind me and hit my shoulder. "*Shhh.*" I snickered. As we moved through the crowd of partygoers toward the private elevator in the back of the building, we grabbed a few attractive strangers to join us. I got the attention of my DJ friend, D-Nice, with a 'what's up' nod. I'd been a fan since the 90's and was fortunate enough to befriend him a few years ago. Our elevated private area had a balcony with a dual view of the 7th Avenue on the outside and view of the entire club inside. Drinks were flowing and so was the love. "Shout out to the only female crew that matters! My girl Desiree is in the house! I see you, babe!" D-Nice's voice echoed over a low beat. I leaned over the banister just enough to give a pageant girl wave then blew a kiss in his direction. My friends and I were all smiles. This was a good, no, great night! Happiness had found me again, but this time in the form of badassness.

Tonight was about Desi. For the next hour, we danced until our hearts content and flirted with several men. Everyone was doing their own thing. The vibe was good until I noticed Tina disappeared. I got an uneasy feeling in the pit of my stomach. I stopped dancing and tapped Tara on the shoulder and asked where Tina had gone. She shrugged her shoulders and kept dancing. I searched the club for her image. Just then, we saw a huge crowd of moving toward a corner of the dance floor. Hair was being pulled and fists were flying. From where we stood we could see two burly security guards separating the pair.

"That is so classless!" Angel said.

"Urgh! Who does that!" Tara twisted her face and hit my arm.

"Ouch! What was that for?" I said hitting her back.

"Girl! That's Tina!"

"No, it isn't," I said taking another look. To my surprise, it *was* Tina! "What the hell!"

All five of us took off downstairs to the first floor. By the time we'd gotten close enough for us to verify that it was our friend, the same security that escorted us in was escorting Tina out. We followed them just outside the entrance of the building.

"You guys don't have to leave but *she*," he pointed to Tina, who was in a full rant, "has to go!"

My face turned red as I tried to contain my embarrassment and anger. "What happened?"

"You ok?" Trisha asked Tina.

"Fighting! Really?" Sasha chastised.

"We're grown women!" Angel scolded.

"Who fights in a club!" Tara squeaked.

"Especially *this* one! I know these people! You just embarrassed me!" I barked.

"So nobody is gonna ask how I'm doing? I didn't start the damn fight! *That* bitch did!" Tina yelled pointing to another woman with wild hair and missing an extension.

"Okay fine! Why are *two* grown women in a nice establishment like this, fighting like two ghetto girls! *Why?*" I demanded.

"I was minding my own business and she walked by me and pushed me." Tina started to explain.

"*She pushed you*," Sasha repeated.

"Yes! *Pushed me!* So I pushed her back and she pulled my hair, I punched her and – "

"Stop! Just stop it! I don't want to hear anymore!" I turned to go back inside the club. "Ladies, are you coming?" I had said before I walked through the door.

"Desi, we can't leave her out here alone." Angel pleaded.

"Yes, we can! And yes I will! I have to go apologize to D and Eric for this. *She* was the one that got kicked out. Why should I mess up my night?!"

"Desi, that's fucked up!" Tina shouted.

"Shut up!" I shouted back. I walked back inside and beckoned for Eric.

"Are you guys ok?" He asked with sincere concern.

"Yes. I'm so sorry."

"No. No. Not your fault."

As I was speaking to Eric, Sasha came to my side, then Trisha, Angel, and finally Tara. We were all there except Tina. "What did you guys do with her?"

"I gave her the keys and told her I would catch a ride with one of you."

"Good idea!" I low fived Angel.

Tina stomped her way back to the parking garage. She pulled out her cell phone and text; '*This place is dead. I'm sure I'd have more fun with you.*' Seconds later a message appeared; '*Will you now…*' She responded quickly, '*I'm on my way. Where are you?*' The phone beeped again with an address. Tina giggled and sped away.

YOU CAME TOO

I arrived home to an empty house. There was a note of the refrigerator from J.J. that read;

I CANNOT AND WILL NOT LIVE LIKE THAT! YOU WILL NOT ACT THE WAY YOU DID BEFORE YOU LEFT HERE EVER AGAIN. YOU ARE MY WIFE NOT SOME TRICK OFF THE STREET AND YOU BETTER START ACTING LIKE YOU KNOW THAT I LOVE YOU! I WILL NOT TALK ABOUT THIS MATTER ANY FURTHER. WHEN YOU HAVE COME TO YOUR SENSES AND APOLOGIZE, I WILL FORGIVE YOU. BUT NEVER AGAIN WILL YOU DESTROY OUR HOME OR LAY A FINGER ON ME. GOT IT! YOUR HUSBAND, JAMES

I took the note down and threw it in the trash. It angered me at first, but I made up my mind not channel my inner bad girl when things between James and I got rough. If I could do that, I could do anything! My house was quiet, too quiet. I didn't expect J.J. to walk through the door anytime soon and I was tired from traveling. The issue with Tina was still on my mind, but I guess she was okay because the whole flight home she kept looking into the air and smiling. I didn't have much to say to her ever since the club incident. Funny how the two most important people in my life managed to make me the most outraged and miserable in a matter of days and each wanted me to fix the situation first. I contemplated my next move in each situation from my favorite thinking spot, the bay window.

It was a dreary morning. You know the kind of day that makes you want to crawl to the center of your bed, get underneath the covers and pretend that it is still night outside. But instead, I reached for the faux fur blanket that was stretched along the back of the couch, wrapped it around me, put on my fury bear claw slippers, propped the pillows up against one side of the bay window in the living room and scooted on the cushion, knees bent, in a sitting fetal position. I leaned my head to one side and started to imagine the rain (or the inclement weather that appeared to be coming) falling at that angle. Then I tried to imagine life without me in it. I couldn't. Not because I didn't try, but because these losers I call family and friends wouldn't be anything if I weren't there to give them my special brand of love. That thought plastered a smile on my face so wide that I laughed out loud. I straightened my neck and stared at the house across the street. Someone was in the window there too! I guess I wasn't the only one with an early morning problem. So I watched.

It was a woman I'd never seen before. I squinted as I tried to make out her full figure from five hundred yards way. Aw, what the hell, I needed binoculars. Without turning my head, I reached for the pair resting on the shelf under the coffee table. I might as well have a little fun. I placed them on my face and immediately giggled at what I saw. The woman, whom I'd never seen before had her back against the window. She was butt bald naked. She was using her hands as balancing bars against the window seat. Her breast bounced in slow motion and her knees were bent and spread apart. I admired her skin and the pointed toes that let me know that whatever she was doing - she was definitely enjoying! Her head was slightly tilted back and I could tell she was seductively moaning because she would lick her lips with the tip of her tongue with every other movement. Damn! Her lips were so very suckable! I was so into the free porn that was in front of me that I started to feel aroused. I was dying to see who or what was giving her such pleasure. I decided it had to be a great vibrator or a man with a really great tongue. I panned down with the binoculars and noticed the top of a head moving in a bobbing motion. *Mmmm.* I moaned and arched my back. The head slowed down and then stop. It just paused. Right there, in the middle of her – I'm sure now – throbbing, pussy. Hers had to be because mine was doing the same – pulsing so hard I reached down and started to roll my small, elongated pearl between my thumb and forefinger. I moaned louder.

My wetness started to feel like a warm pool of honey, thick and sticky. One hand still on the binoculars, I focused harder on the head that provided so much pleasure. I must know who this is. The head started moving again. It moved up and out and licked and kissed the lower belly of the mystery woman. My eyes grew large. That's when I noticed the head was attached to a woman! She was naked and on her knees. She placed her hands on either side of the mystery woman's waist as the mystery woman released her other hand from the top of her head. I'm not gay at all. Never have been! But for some reason this turned me on even more! The way she was kissing and caressing the body in the window was all about pleasure. The knee lady glanced my direction, gave the window lady a full mouth kiss and glanced back at me again. I didn't move. I just kept touching myself until my finger had a mind of its own. I was so wet that the hand motion of my various strokes made squishing sounds that echoed in the room. I was sure the knee lady saw me. She had to. But I wasn't going to stop until they did. I had ! With an unwavering dedication to the real life porn movie we all seemed to be involved in, I slumped down further under my blanket to adjust my position, never once taking my eyes off my prize.

A man, whom I recognized as my neighbor, Anthony, entered the picture. *Oh, this keeps getting better!* I laughed inside. While the women continued to deep mouth each other he slapped his long, thick, brown dick on the back of the knee ladies butt – who, by the way, was no longer on her knees – she stood to bend and kiss the window lady. With one motion, he kissed knee ladies shoulder and slide inside of her. She let out a big *"OOOO"* as he grabbed her shoulders to gain control by holding on and penetrated her from behind. First fast. Then slow. Then medium. Then fast again. She was in such ecstasy that she'd stopped kissing the window lady in the mouth. No, now she'd spread her legs to lower herself just enough to place her face back into the window lady's pleasure palace while the window lady fondled her breast with both hands. I screeched a little as my body heated up into a small sweat. This felt dirty. It felt weird but in a right kind of way. I liked it! I wanted to try it! I wanted to have it! I'd gone from one finger to two and rubbed it so hard that I could feel the sensation of my orgasm enlarge. I remembered then – this is what squirting is supposed to feel like. I'd read a book about pleasuring yourself that it was possible for women to have such large orgasms that the fluid literally squirts out of you. *WOW!* This was the greatest, most exciting feeling!

He banged her fast, I massaged my pussy fast. He went in slow and deep, I went in slow and deep. I could still see the knee lady look my direction from time to time and I could only imagine the sounds in that room. I was the window lady! She was I and I was her. The two ladies switched positions. Still seated in the window, he penetrated the now writhing window lady from the front while the knee lady sucked her breast and played with her clit. His delivery with the window lady was undoubtedly different. He was paced and steady with her. Every move Anthony made was intentional, he was certain to go as deep as he could to extract the maximum amount of pleasure out of her. She stared into his eyes and he into hers. The knee lady was so into her actions that I don't think she noticed how deep the other two participants were. I mouthed a supple, "I love this." to him and he mouthed it back. Once she lifted her legs to rest on his shoulders, she gyrated in a counter clockwise motion. It must have felt amazing because even I could see his knees get weak. I-I couldn't take it any longer. I let out the loudest scream that I'd ever heard and every ounce of fluid inside me came rushing out and onto the seat cushion and blanket.

Release.

KNOCK KNOCK

I couldn't stop thinking about Raymond. How he felt and how alive I felt with him. After several days of secret phone calls and rendezvous, I gave in. He asked me to meet him at his home for dinner and a little conversation. When I accepted the invitation, I had no intention to of eating anything. The only conversation I wanted to have was how and where he was going to take advantage of me.

I found the key to his house under the rug, just as he'd instructed. I unlocked the door and went inside. I looked around at the décor, art deco. *Impressive choice,* I thought as I admired the elegant, strong geometric forms, and eclectic motifs with rich, saturated displayed art but neutral colors everywhere else.

The entryway was laid with dark oak hardwood which led to the carpeted living room, where the walls were beige with heather gray trim on the baseboards and around the doorways. The furniture consisted of a single red mesh sofa and a matching beige love seat, both bearing the S-curve and on each rested two silk throw pillows. The coffee and end tables were round in shape. I concluded that they came from the same tree as the floor because they were an exact match. In the bay window accented with multicolored silk curtains, stood one tall lamp, a tiny reading table and chocolate brown leather chair with a red silk pillow lying on its arm. There was no television, the centerpiece of the room was the brown, white and beige marble fireplace outlined in dark oak and holding up an enormous curved mirror. The curvilinear shape of the sexiest stare case I'd ever seen stood out as an exhibit, it was almost waving at me. The banister, with its alternating dark oak and white limbs, virtually swayed its ways up the side of the rounded corners of the polished dark oak stairs with accents of white in between each step. The white walls seemed to add brightness to the dark places that led to the second floor. The door to a small bathroom was open and I could see the all-white motif.

The two paintings that hung on the wall where I stood in the living room stared back at me from either side. In one, there was a young woman wearing a big white floppy hat, with one white-gloved hand holding the tip of its brim. Her eyes were green and her hair was a curly brown. Her lips were a shade of red and her mouth was closed tight. Her dress was the shade of her eyes and her complexion was light brown. It must've been cold when the artist painted her picture because her nipples protruded through the folds of ruffles in the sleeveless dress against the black, white and beige background. The other painting was also of a woman. She was peering at me from all angles in a white one strap sleeveless dress – one arm crossed the breast area as she cupped a bouquet of white orchids. There was red fabric swaddled around and entangled between the large green leaves of the orchids. I took a moment to admire the size of each model. They were thick by urban standards and portrayed the beauty of the average woman.

Looking at the imagery made me feel sexy. I peeled off my skirt and fitted waist blouse but decided to keep my black Betsy Johnson five inch heels on. In my pink and yellow lace bra and boy shorts, I performed a slow model walk up the stairs into the bedroom. I felt sexier with each step. I sauntered my way into the bedroom closet and pulled the double doors toward me. I stood with my legs slightly spread apart and placed my hands on my hips, cocked my head to the left, and licked my peach glosses lips with the tip of my tongue from right to left all the way around. I bit the tip of my index finger, *which of his shirts and ties and I going to slip into. Hmmm.* I sifted through each of the men's shirts all neatly pressed and hung just so when my eyes happened upon the lone football jersey resting in the back of the closet, almost hidden from plain sight. Leaning forward, I reached for this prized item and quickly withdrew my hand. I looked down at and admired my body. I liked the way my armed looked, the extension made every inch of my caramel brown skin ooze with sex. My breast stood full and tight in my specialty bra and the diamond pendant hanging from the pink bow on my yellow lace underwear glimmered in the light. I touched myself. I ran my hand over my chest then down my stomach, stopping just before I reached my now increasingly wet kitty. I took a deep breath and allowed my hands to continue on its journey, extending a single finger between the lips where my throbbing pink pearl awaited. I rolled my finger hard and in circles until my entire body reacted with an intense lurch forward that. I moaned with delight and widened the half smile on my face. I pulled my finger away from the rhythm long enough to taste myself. Without a second thought, I grabbed the jersey from the back of the closet off the hanger, pulled off my underwear and unsnapped my bra with one hand and let them fall to the floor. Next I pulled off each heel they clunked as they dropped to the floor in front of the closet. My heart rate increased with each passing moment. A long slow breath escaped my body just as I pulled the jersey over my head and down the curves of my body. It was too big and too long but seemed to fit every silky inch of me like a glove. I melted as I fell back on the bed. I spread my legs into a butterfly position where my perfectly manicured toes met. I allowed my hips and thighs to relax, letting each leg to fall further to its respective side. I liked this feeling. I was free. No inhibitions. No worries. No feelings of shame at all, just a fantastically great sense of freedom. I finally let go. I was finally ok with me.

I was engulfed in my own personal ecstasy before I realized I was in full climax and my fingers we moving fast in and out of my great divide. I screamed his name, rolled around in his bed and poured all of my feminine juices all over his sheets.

I continued to breathe heavily through my screams of pleasure without a care of who might have overheard me. My naked body lay comfortably under the blanket of his jersey. I took one last breath and fell swiftly to sleep in the middle of his bed, wearing his jersey – wet sheets and all.

I wasn't sure how long I'd been asleep, but when I woke, Ray was sitting on the side of the bed wearing nothing and looking at me. He steadied himself with one hand across my hips and traced my face with his fingers. I didn't move. He kissed my bottom lip twice. I reached up and wrapped my arms around his neck. I kissed him hard and as deep as he'd allowed me to. I wanted him to know that I was here for him. I was risking a lot to be here and he needed to know that I wanted him as much as he wanted me. We pulled away from each other, I took his hand and placed it on my other set of lips and bent one finger inside my passage. He closed his eyes, inhaled, and wiggled his finger to get a reaction out of me. I adjusted my hips and slightly arched my back just enough to feel the thickness of his fingers.

Ray repositioned himself without removing his finger from my center. He landed on top of me with his full weight. For some reason, the pressure was of his body made his finger feel deeper, thicker and more amazing. I moved my legs to fit the width of his body between my legs and he adjusted accordingly. "What are you waiting for?" I said in soft voice.

"I can't believe you're here."

"Believe it. I am."

"Don't ever leave me. It's been too long." He confessed.

"I won't. I promise." I lied. I knew I had to go home to my husband. I also knew I wasn't sure of Ray's motives. Until I figured it out, I decided to just live in the moment of lust. He raised his hips and I took hold of the massiveness that was his manhood and gradually inserted him inside of me. He moved his the pelvis in circles as he lay on top of me. My first climax came quickly. Sex with Ray was soothing and purposeful and...unbelievably exciting! We fit together too well! There was so much chemistry between us we could stimulate each other with our eyes. He took his time with me, something I can say James had forgotten about over the past few years. The moans in the room bounced off the walls and resounded in our ears as they grew louder and louder and louder until, "RAY!!!!!!" He clinched my body and let out a flow that I felt inside my walls, and then pulled himself out and off of me.

"I'm not through with you yet," He said flopping on the side of me.

"If you think I'm done with you, you are sadly mistaken, sir," I said honestly.

"Tell me your deepest fantasy," He said sucking my nipples.

"Well..." I found myself blushing, "I watched someone have a threesome, two girls, and one guy. I've always wanted to try it." I admitted. "And...." I bit my tongue.

"Go on." He encouraged.

"Ever since the club, I wanted to try anal again," I confessed.

"I think I can help you with both of those." He offered confidently, kissing my belly.

"How does that work? The threesome, I mean?"

"You get three people and do what comes naturally or unnaturally at the time," He explained.

I giggled at his explanation and he got up from the bed and went into the bathroom. He left the door open while he peed. He leaned back to continue to continue our conversation. "Your wish is my command. I will set the whole thing up." He said shaking his penis and wiping it dry.

"Should I study for this exam?"

He walked into the closet and pulled something from the top shelf. He handed me a book full of sexual position and exploration. I didn't want to open it in front of him, but I took the hint.

"How was your day?" He asked with genuine interest.

"Wet." I responded and rolled on my stomach. Something about that statement brought his member back to life because before I could get comfortable he was rubbing his dick on my ass.

"Let's try that anal thing again."

"Only if you have lube."

"I'm not going to lie, anal sex is 50% pleasure and 50% pain for the woman. I want you to be comfortable, so ask me anything you want before we try it again. If you know what to expect, then you will know when or if to tell me to stop." He reassured me.

"Um…okay…other than lube do I need to do anything else? You are on the large side." I pointed.

"First, you have to have lots of trust when it comes to this – trust *and* patience. I'm not going to lie, it is going to hurt, but you already know that. You have to find a way to make yourself comfortable. Take it easy, 'cause if you rush it, that's when it's gonna hurt."

I tensed my butt muscles and started to rethink my request. I'm sure he'd enjoy it, and some women would prefer not to do it, but I was not that woman. I left that woman somewhere on the coast. It hurts. Let me tell you, it hurts *really* badly. "I thought I was ready but now…."

Ceasing the opportunity to fulfill his kinky craving Ray swore, "With enough lube you won't even feel a thing. Pain only means stopping. Not withdrawing, but stopping. Just focus on your breathing, and I will do the rest. I'm home now, I'm prepared." He opened a drawer on the nightstand and pulled out a bottle of KY gel and lathered his dip stick while kissing my back. "Here comes daddy," He said sliding in my behind. Ray started to caress other areas of my body in an attempt to relax my muscles.

Nothing is supposed to go in the anus, nothing! Not even your soul mates genitalia, nothing!

After we had gotten past the point of me relaxing enough for Ray to get inside, the sex was amazing! My back arched with a small curve and he was able to go a little deeper. My legs quivered when I felt his extension in my stomach, and my eyes rolled. I gripped either side of the bed in an attempt to control the uncontrollable. Well, it was painful at the beginning, and at the end, in the middle it was somewhat enjoyable. Lubrication was the key and getting me relaxed was the main thing! For Ray, it was pure sex and gave him the most intense orgasm. To put it simply, things aren't supposed to go in there, but I've had the experience and now I'm satisfied.

THE OTHER....UM...

I'm struggling with some things in my life. All these sad and disturbing things keep crossing my mind. I think I want to see other people. And why do I feel so free when I'm with Raymond and so restricted when I'm with James. I want a new hair style, a new job and a cruise to some exotic place. Sounds like a midlife crisis but it's not nearly the middle of my life! I keep having these feelings that I want to explore other men and women sexually. Curiosity killed the cat and I still have all my nine lives. I used to think that I couldn't do that – That my conscience would eat me alive. Plus I'm afraid of secrets. My husband is safe. I'm afraid of uncertainty. My life was safe.

James and I started to lead the lives of single people. I'd walk into the house and he'd walk out. I'd go to our bedroom and he'd go to the guest room. He stayed out until all hours of the morning and I did the same. We never spoke – not verbally at least. We communicated through posted notes and email only when absolutely necessary.

Meanwhile, Raymond and I were spending more time together. I read the book of sexual positions he'd given me to study. I learned more about myself from reading that book than I'd ever imagined. We discussed our fantasies and concerns about exploring them. I confided in him about the problems in my marriage and he listened. Ray made me feel better about the whole situation. If I were to ever leave my husband, he would be there to step into my life permanently. In a bold attempt to test the waters of our relationship feasibility elected to spend the next couple days with Ray at his home. I packed a bag and left a note on the counter telling J.J. he had the house to himself for awhile.

The moment I arrived at Ray's place, I was comfortable. Before I could get out of the car, he flung open the front door and said, "Welcome home babe!" He brought my bags inside and took them to his bedroom where a massage therapist waited for us. He wasted no time getting me undressed and onto the table. "I want you to relax and make yourself at home." He took my hand and squeezed. All I could do was squeeze back.

Later that evening, I pulled his book from my purse and sat it on the coffee table. He looked at it, then at me with a raised eyebrow. "If we are going to try everything in that book, we'd better get started. I'm only here for a limited time." I smiled and sat on his lap. My kisses must have excited him because he didn't bother going to the bedroom, he took me right then and there on the living room floor. We made love for hours in the missionary position. It was slow and deliberate and intense.

Every time he thought he was going to cum, he paused to let the sensation die down. I never knew the missionary position could be that…intense! I fell asleep in his arms in the middle of the living room floor.

The next day, we had breakfast and bathed together. He spared no time getting me sweaty all over again. I let him have sex with me anally. I let him cum in my mouth, tie me up, and penetrate both orifices at the same time. By then I felt comfortable enough to make a request – I wanted to have a ménage à trios with him and another female. He sat back and studied me closely. "Are you sure you're ready for that?"

"Yes," I said emphatically.

"Let me make a call. I think we can handle that."

"So you just keep chicks on speed dial for this type of thing?" I asked seriously.

"No. I just know someone that is ready for that kind of thing."

"So you've used her before?"

"You make it sound so dirty. She's not a prostitute. She is someone I trust."

"Have you ever been in a relationship with this woman?"

"Nope. We had fun a couple of times over the years…but that's the only time I see her."

"So you call each other for this kinda thing!" I squawked. "I think I'm changing my mind."

"Don't be scared. When you are a bachelor, you just know people. That's all. Let me call her. If you change your mind after she gets here, then we won't do it. But at least give it the old college try before you miss out on the experience of a lifetime." He dialed the phone.

Oddly enough, what he said made sense. I thought about my neighbor and his window experience and how much I was into what was going on. And how he was in tune with the main girl but managed to incorporate the other woman strictly for excitement and pleasure. When the woman arrived about an hour later, I was all in! I didn't want to know her name, nor did I want her to know mine, so we agreed to call each other *'Girl X.'* She wore a tight red dress with heels that brought her eight inches closer to heaven. I was turned on simply, by the way, she strutted through the foyer and sat on the arm of the couch with perfect posture. Ray planted a kiss on her cheek and handed us glasses of wine. I wanted her to touch me first because I wasn't sure if it was okay for me to touch her first. She must've read my mind because she put down her glass and came to me. Ray stood by and watched the nervousness on my face develop. Like the true gentlemen he was, he stepped in to save me. He moved her aside and kissed me and assured me that I had total control to start or stop the situation at will. I shook my head in agreement and took her hand as I walked toward the bedroom.

"Show me." Girl X said.

"Show you what?" I questioned.

"Show her." Ray encouraged me.

"Can I see your nipples?" Girl X asked.

"Can I touch you?" An internal flame

consumed me.

We touched each other a lot; I think that was the most exciting part. She was gentle when needed and forceful when warranted. Ray was careful not to penetrate her, although I could tell he really wanted to, "You are the most important person in this room and I need you to know that." He whispered in my ear. I felt bad that Girl X wouldn't get the benefit of a real flesh, so I asked Ray to invite someone else to take care of it for her. She placed a finger over my lips and pulled out the largest toy I'd ever seen and said, "I'm just here because I like to have fun. I've got this. You just enjoy yourself." I wasn't finished, but then I realized I had to stop somewhere.

When it was all over, I thought it would be corny to thank you so the only thing I could think to say was, "I like the dimples on your back."

"Thanks!" She winked and left Ray and me alone.

"So…how do you feel?" Ray asked leaning over me.

"Sexy!" I responded.

"You're already sexy, anything else?" He traced my body with his fingers.

"Okay…liberated!"

"Now that's better." He kissed me. "I don't let these little things slip out of my mouth….I'm in love with you." He professed.

I was swept up in the intensity of the moment and responded with, "I love you too Raymond Humphrey!" Not sure of what else to say, I got up from the bed and went into the bathroom,

"Stop looking at my ass!" I laughed.

Raymond was good! *Oh*, he was good! Always saying, doing little things to keep my attention and gain my trust. Eventually, I gave in. All those things add up and after a while I got weak. Now I'm here, sick to my stomach asking, *how did we get here*. How did we get to the point where we're sending pictures, masturbating, having orgies, kissing and saying, *I love you*. How did we get here? When did scary become safe? What was the date – the time that said, *yes this is wrong but oh so right?*

We slept like babies that night, except every other hour Ray woke me by burying his face in my yoni. He was relentless! He only stopped when he could feel my climax on his face. He didn't try inserting himself inside me once, just ate me out all night long. The last round had me so hot that in a frenzied rush I screamed, "I love you, James!"

Ray stopped mid motion and sat up straight. "James?"

"Oh my god…Ray…I- I…" I couldn't explain.

Ray got angry. "Listen, you better decided right now if you're my woman or his wife!" He left the room and I followed behind him.

"Ray….Ray, you've got to understand that I've been with one man and one man only…until now. I can't just erase every trace of him from my life overnight. It's going to take some time. I'm sorry."

"*Sorry?* You yelled another man's name! That means you were thinking of him while I was pleasing you!"

"No, it doesn't Ray! It means this is the first time I've made that mistake and that I felt comfortable enough to call out anyone's name and the only name I had ever called out was his!"

"I don't want to hear you calling his name! All I want to know is do you love me and if you do; don't ever make that mistake again!"

"You know I do! I'm sorry. Now come back to bed and stop ruining my visit." I kissed Ray's cheek. We went back to bed, but he held me extra tight and extra close that night. He knew I would be leaving in the morning, but I wasn't sure if I was coming back.

I hadn't heard from Tina since we came home and it was really starting to bother me. I picked up the phone to call her but hung up before it could ring. I'd heard from Sasha and Tara that Tina made a new friend in Florida and had been spending lots of time with her. I figured if that was the way she wanted it, then so be it. Tina took a much-needed break from our friendship and made some choices that apparently made her happy. I guess my choices had affected her in a way I didn't even realize. During a lunch date, Tina and her new friend discussed exploring a wilder side of life together.

"Life is too short for me not to have a little fun!" Tina laughed.

"Listen, my life is what I make it. I do who and what I want to, with no strings attached." Girl X asserted. "Take the other night for example. A friend of mine called me to help him break his new girl into a freakier side of life. I figured hell, why not, I was bored and he always kept it interesting. So I go over to his place and she was sitting there looking all scared and timid. But we worked it out. I got to play and he got to get off."

"So what you're saying is you're in the business of breaking people in," Tina said intrigued.

"No, not in the business, more like a hobby. I only get down when I feel like it and it turned out that night I was ready for a new challenge. What can I say, I'm a free spirit!"

"I see! I'm bold but not that damn bold."

"You starting to sound like you might want to get broke in too." Girl X peered at Tina.

"Maybe it's time for something different," Tina answered.

"Uh-huh....Well, I could make a phone call and see what's poppin'."

"Nothing wrong with making a phone call." Tina smiled.

"Be right back." Girl X excused herself and dialed Ray's phone number. "Hello."

"What's up sweetie," Ray answered.

"Nothing much....I've got a favor to ask."

"Anything for you. I already owe you big." Ray said.

"You know how I helped your situation the other night?"

"Yeah."

"I need you to return the favor. My new friend wants to experience to 2 to 1 ratio."

Ray sighed, "I don't know sweetie. I'm really feeling my girl...."

"You owe me, Ray! Plus why would I call anybody else, I know you're safe." Girl X said.

Ray took a long pause. " 'Aight, just this once."

"You won't regret it! I promise! Wait, does your new girl mean I have to find new playmates?"

"Maybe. I need to see where this goes." Ray answered with a smile.

"Gotcha! See you later tonight!" Girl X said hanging up the phone. She approached the table where Tina sat. "Good news! We've got a date tonight!"

"This should be interesting!" Tina high fived her. "I haven't done this since college."

I woke up to a text from Ray:

"I had a long nite Friday and got up late. This whole thing weekend was crazy and this one coming will be the same. Lots of bday parties @ clubs."

I texted him back a simple, *"OK. Have fun!"* and went about my day.

TRUTH BE TOLD

Days had gone by since I last saw my husband. I kept replaying the incident with Ray in my head. I really did want the tongue that gave me such pleasure to be my husband's. I really was thinking about J.J. when I called his name. I missed him and his touch. After a couple of days of playing house with Ray, things began to remind me of James. Just when I thought I was over it, I'm right back to where I started...missing him. There was no contact whatsoever between us, so I sent him a message:

I love you. We need to seriously talk. Come home or pick up the phone and let's stop being stubborn.

I closed my laptop and dialed the phone, "Hey D!" Tara's perky voice resounded.

"Hey, girl! Whatcha up to?" I said trying to sound upbeat.

"Nothing. Sipping on some wine and watching a movie." Tara said.

"Oh, well, in that case, I will cut right to the chase....I'm super sad. I'm trying not to cry and I don't know what do to about my marriage." I admitted.

"Aw D. I'm so sorry hun. You want to talk about it?" Her concern was comforting.

"The not talking is the worst" I came clean. "I don't care if he tells me to go to hell, just tell me something. Ya' know." My eyes watered.

"You are gonna have to give it time if you want to fix your relationship. Not your time, though. Maybe you both need to learn something from this. You can't fix what you don't think is broken and this whole experience showed a crack in your relationship." Tara advised.

"Maybe you're right. I just don't know how long I can keep going like this."

"Desiree, don't get in your own way," Tara warned.

I understood my friend was giving me advice based on the information I'd given her so I couldn't truly defend my position. "It all looks like it is, doesn't it."

"Yes, it does. Unless there is something you aren't telling me." Tara pressed.

"No. Or at least nothing I'm willing to come clean about right now. I'm still in the stage of making horrible decisions about my marriage that I think will bring me closer to a resolution." The hurt started to subside when a moment of clarity washed over her like a cold summer rain. "I need to remove the cancer from my life. I can't be his friend...I love him too much. Short of him getting with Beyonce I wouldn't be able to stand it. And even then I would find a flaw or two or three."

"Desi? Are you talking to yourself or me?" Tara asked unsure of the turn the conversation had taken.

Ignoring Tara all together, I said, "I need a fresh start. I need a new place to forget all of this. But where?" And hung up the phone. I sat on the couch for another hour and searched my email on my smartphone for some sign that he'd acknowledged my message. Nothing. "I'm done! I can't take this shit! I feel like a crazy person." I screamed at the top of my lungs as I whipped a crystal wine glass across the room. Stunned into silence, I stood in the middle of the living room staring wide-eyed at the shattered glass crashing to the floor. I felt a single tear slide over my left dimple and fall from my round checks to the carpet. I stood motionless as a feeling of complete numbness traveled throughout my body beginning with my toes. My mind raced. Confused and disoriented there was nothing left to do but cry. I had never experienced hatred until now. "I think I hate him," I mumbled. When the trance was finally broken, I sat in the window and made myself a promise.

The next afternoon, I went to Raymond's house to tell him that I wanted to work on my marriage and we should stop seeing each other before things got serious. He was angry all over again. I tried to calm him down, but he was not the gentlemen that I knew him to be. He had this look in his eyes that scared me. That's when it became clear that he was more serious about this than I was.

"Why are we fighting? This is stupid!" I

shouted.

"Shut up and fuck me!" Ray demanded.

"Sex won't fix this Ray! I've got to make this right if I can." I pleaded.

"You didn't fuck up your marriage Desi! He did! Why would you want to fix that?" I hollered. The garage door was open and it was quiet outside so the argument echoed. I followed behind him yelling.

"If I wanted to fight I would have stayed at home with my husband!"

He stopped dead in his tracks and turned to look her sharply in the eyes. "Listen to me clearly! I don't give a flying fuck about your husband! Don't ever mention his name around me again."

Wide-eyed and shocked by his abrupt assertion, I froze but managed to blink. I'd never seen his him react this way. He was always so smooth and nonchalant about everything. "Ray," I said calmly. "This is too intense for me right now. We need to think about this with clear heads."

"What do you need me to make clearer for you Desi? I love you! You! I've never loved anybody, ever! And I love you! Now you're standing in front of me telling me that you want to work things out with your –"

"Husband. Say it Ray. My husband. No matter what we say or do right now, the fact is I'm still very married." I professed. "I do love you, Ray. I also love my husband and I made a promise to him first. I don't expect you to understand, but I *have* to do this."

"Fine." He rubbed his eyes. "Just know I

won't be her forever. I'm a man and I've got needs too."

"Then it's settled." I turned and left his house. Ray had the power of persuasion on his side. The kind that could make you follow him into a burning building but this time I didn't.

READY OR NOT

After reading my message several times, James come to the conclusion that he needed to accept responsibility for the problems he and I faced. It was time to let the problem go. J.J. parked his car on the street two blocks away from Smith & Wollensky restaurant. As he walked toward the dimly lit outdoor patio, he recited his prepared let down speech. He decided to meet *'the mistake'* here, on the other side of town. He figured it would be safer than meeting anywhere near his home or social network. The hostess directed him to the woman in wait and he took his seat across from her. She was excited to see him and flattered at his choice of restaurant.

"Listen, we need to talk."

"I'm listening honey."

"I just wanted to tell you that we need to stop seeing each other. You are a lovely woman and I really appreciate you for who you are, but I need some time to work on myself."

"You brought me here to break up with me?" She said angrily.

"Break up?" He said baffled. "We were never in *that* kind of relationship. I thought you understood that we were friends, not lovers. That one time was a mistake." He clarified.

"*Mistake,*" She repeated.

"Yes. A mistake. I like you as a person but nothing more."

"So why did you string me along all this time?"

"I didn't string you along!" J.J. said more puzzled. "I have a wife. You know that!"

"You mean the woman who you've been dodging. That wife."

"Hey! That is none of your business! I wanted to let you down easy, but you're going too far." He gritted his teeth.

"Fine Mr. Taylor. Have it your way." She said sitting back in her chair.

"Good. I hope we can agree that there is no need to get ugly about this." His corporate demeanor reared its head.

"No. You won't have any problems with me." She said confidently.

"I have to go, but order what you want and have it billed to me," James said standing.

"Goodbye James." She waved.

James walked through dining area of the restaurant and into the men's room. When he walked in Raymond stared him down. Already in a foul mood, James snapped at him, "What are you looking at?"

"A nobody." Ray snapped back.

"Excuse me! Have we met?" J.J.'s chest swelled.

"Naw. I know you but you sure in the hell

don't know me!" Ray said drying his hands on a paper towel.

James sized him up, "Man, tonight is not the night for you to test your manhood!"

"Oh trust me, I'm not testing my manhood. I never have to, unlike some people." Ray stood firm.

"What the fuck are you talking about?" J.J. finally asked.

"I'm talking about Desiree," Ray said with a raised brow.

"Did my wife send you here to spy on me?" James asked.

"Naw man, I'm just a concerned citizen. See, you don't know what you have. Do you know how many men would kill for a woman like her?" Ray said.

"I do now. Let me take care of this side." James tried to sound secure.

"You better! There's a line behind me waiting for you to fuck up! And from where I stand, you are doing a bang up job!" Ray said crossing his arms.

"How do you know my wife?" J.J. jaw tightened.

"Let's just say she is a very dear friend that I like to spend a lot of time with." Ray smiled. "I don't feel bad for people like you. You're so smart you're stupid! Keep up the good job! Saying 'I do' has nothing to do with meaning it. You can't leave her in a marriage alone and not expect her to go along with it." Ray stared James down.

"As long as you not fucking me wife what

the fuck do you care?!" James insisted.

"Who said I haven't." Ray proclaimed and walked out of the bathroom.

J.J. was furious. *Who the hell was that and how did he know so much about my marriage?* He took off after Ray, who was standing in front of the restaurant waiting for the valet to deliver his car. "You son-of-a-bitch!" J.J. said punching Ray in the jaw. Ray fell stumbled backward, "Stay the hell away from my wife!" James shouted as another valet put him in a full Nelson hold. Ray recovered his footing and laughed at J.J.

"Let the poor man go," Ray instructed the valet. "He just got the caught cheating on his wife. His night was bad enough already." Ray continued laughing as he got into his car and drove away.

It was a quarter after nine when I pulled my SUV into my designated parking spot at the office building where I worked. The gated parking lot appeared to be empty. My parking spot was a little distance from the building, but there is something to be said for being a creature of habit. It was dark out, but the moonlight managed to show off of the freshly repaved blacktop pavement.

"Good. I can do what I have to do and get out of here." I said to no one, as I shifted the car into park. I paused for a moment because I felt someone's eyes staring at me. I locked the doors and looked around – never taking my foot off the break in case I had to shift quickly to get out of there. The moon roof of my car was still open so I could hear the outside clearly. I glanced down at my car radio, it read 9:29 p.m. *Hmmm.* I hesitated and shrugged off the peeping-Tom feeling as I turned off the engine and exited my vehicle. I moved my legs slightly apart and my left heel hit the ground with a quick *clack*. My bare oiled legs and lower body felt the warm air slide pass. I grinned slightly and patted myself on the back because I decided not to wear any panties. Going natural had become my thing. This is the kind of deliberate decision making that made me feel sexy and oddly powerful. The breeze seemed to cool my inner thighs and tickle my middle enough to make me giggle out loud. I pulled the keys from the ignition and looked around once more – nothing, no one.

"Just what are you giggling about?" JJ startled me. I let out a heart-stopping gasp, grabbed my chest, turned around and screamed. "Wait! It's me!" He quickly corrected.

"What the fuck!" I yelled hitting him in the chest with my fist. "Where the hell did you come from?!" I hit him twice more, each blow harder than the last.

"Damn babe! Stop hitting me!" He reached for my arms. "I just wanted to surprise you! Calm down." He said, with his hands on my biceps.

"Don't ever do that! Shit! My heart just jumped out of my chest!" I stomped on his toe with the five-inch heel. He instantly let me go.

"Ouch! Ok! Ok! I know! My bad! Calm down!" He said waving his hands in the air and backing off of me like he was proving he didn't have a weapon.

"What are you doing here?" I demanded.

"I came to surprise you. I miss you and I wanted to see you."

"So you thought your best bet was to stalk me!"

"No. No-It's not like that. I just miss you, babe. I'm sorry."

"For?" I asked.

"Being a dick! Ok! There I said it! I was a dick and I'm sorry."

"Save it, James," I said purposefully dismissing his apology.

"See! That's your motherfuckin' problem right there! Your ass is too damn tough to even accept a sincere ass apology."

"You are something out of a comic book!" My eyes widened in disbelief as I stood with my hands on hips and eyes fixed on his.

"I said I was sorry Desi! That's all I can do right now." J.J. came closer.

"Don't lie! You're not sorry about shit! You are only sorry you got caught! I'm not that chic! So save it!" I crossed my arms over my chest.

"Just come home, D. People-I made a mistake. It wasn't what you think anyway –"

"You are fuckin' kidding me! This is your apology! *It wasn't what I think!*" My yells echoed across the parking lot and J.J. stopped in his tracks and I pushed passed him.

"You are going to stop and listen to me, Desiree Elizabeth Taylor!" He grabbed my forearm and held tight.

"Let me go you stupid son of a bitch!" I

tried to snatch my arm away, but his grip was too tight.

"No! Not until you listen to me." He was relentless.

"Let. Me. Go." My lips pronounced each syllable of each word, so much so that my face seemed to mock my lips. I freed myself.

"I love you, girl!" His tears started to flow. "I can't tell you how bad I messed up, but I think you should at least hear my side of this. You are just as guilty in this as I am. I wasn't in our marriage alone – or was I?" My silence spoke loudly. "Are you listening to me Desi? Give me this. Please!"

I stood motionless. I looked at him like a curious puppy who was trying to understand what was happening. The rush of emotions of fury and fight in me started to calm at the sight of his tears. James Jones Taylor had never once shed a tear in front of me before, never once. His question was like a dagger to my soul.

"That question....Why did you ask *that* question?"

"Is it valid?"

"I-I..." My eyes burned. He came closer.

"We've both had problems with this thing. I love you – I'm in love with you! I know we can work this out. Just give us a chance. You can't say, you gave it your all when –" He spoke fast.

"When what?" I stared at him. I saw his eyes again. The way I used to see them. I felt naked.

"It doesn't matter." He took my hands. "Mistakes were made. We can't take any of it back. But all I know is it's not over for me and you."

"It's not?" My pride refused to let a tear escape. James took that moment to hug me. He took my puffed cheeks in hands and kissed my lips. Leaning his forehead against mine, "I love you D. I love you. I love you."

"Stop it." He kissed my lips again and guided me backward toward the front of the car. I kissed him back.

"Can I have you?" He asked. I nodded.

At that point I decided I didn't want to argue. I didn't want sweet talk or I'm sorry. I just wanted to be loved. So if he was too dumb to understand that then it was my move. With one swift motion, I reached inside his pants, wrapped my hand around his limp dick with one and one around his neck with the other. I maneuvered my body so my now hardened nipples touched his chest. I kissed him deep. "But – I" he started. I kissed him again while finding the vein in the center of his wood with my thumb and stroked. "I gotta – tell you" he continued. My thumb made a circular trace toward the head of his penis. If he was too stupid to shut up and go with it, I was going to make him! I bent the head. He stopped talking. It was my turn to have some fun. I stepped back and looked him in the eyes. He just stood there baffled. I pulled his pants down and squatted in front of him. He was at full attention. His shirt hung over his pole like a towel rack. I clasped both of my hands behind my back and with no hands, tickled the tip with my tongue. I didn't look up. I was laser focused on the task at hand. After a few circles, I went straight up the center, being sure to open the eye of his hard-on.

With my hands still clasped behind my back, I took all of him into my mouth in one motion. I sucked on it like a straw for several moments and allowed all the saliva from my mouth to drip. Then I looked up. Our eyes connected as my jaws flexed. I reached for his nut sack and began to rotate them with one hand. His thighs wavered and my excitement grew. I went deeper with each suck. His dick hit the back of my throat and my gag reflexes kicked in – but I kept going.

MISTAKES COUNT

After J.J. had surprised me with the tear-filled apology, I was convicted to get myself checked out. Just to be sure nothing would prevent my husband and me from repairing our relationship. I remembered watching a movie about a girl that committed suicide because life got to be too much for her, but no one knew she was sad or pregnant. I felt like that girl. I understood her. I went to the drug store and purchased a pregnancy test and an at-home STD testing kit. I figured it would be easier than facing the accusing eyes of my own doctor and nursing staff.

I drank water, pulled hair from the root and swabbed my mouth with perfect certainty that I was not pregnant or contracted any diseases. While I waited for my timer to ding, I cleaned the house and started baking cookies. I was not prepared for the results I got.

My hands shook as I picked up the phone to dial Raymond's number. *Ring. Ring. Ring.*

"Good! Go to voicemail."

Ring.

"Hello." The voice came from the other

end.

"Damn!" I huffed.

"Excuse me?" Raymond quickly responded.

"Oh, sorry I'm driving and someone cut me off." I lied. Not realizing I was calling from my landline.

"You're calling from your house," Ray replied.

"Yeah....um...look we need to talk. Do you have time?

"Yeah go ahead," He said impatiently.

"Well, I think this is a conversation we need to have face to face. Can you get away right now?" I begged.

"Nope." He was short.

"Why?"

"Just say what you have to say."

"The test was positive. Well, one was positive and one was negative."

"What test?!"

"The pregnancy test and HIV test I took."

"Wow."

"Wow...That's all you have to say? This deserves more than a wow, Ray."

"So what you gonna do?" He asked.

"I don't know! I've been trying to get a hold of you for a week. I wanted to do this together."

"Well...."

"You know what! I'll figure it out on my own! I don't want to be bothered with you either!" I yelled." This is hard enough as it is without your drama filled ass."

Dead silence. Ray shut down. I swear he was like a damn deer in headlights.

"Hello!" I shrieked.

"I'll talk to you later," Raymond said flatly.

"Bye." I said coldly and slammed the phone down.

Life at that moment felt so foreign to me. You know how it is when you go someplace and you don't know the language or the culture and everyone looks at you in that "what is she doing here" stare. I kept seeing glaring stares and hearing whispers.

I spotted Tina across the waiting room and breathed and exhausted sigh of relief. Since my conversation with Ray didn't go so well, I wanted to confirm my results with an actual doctor but I had to go to a doctor where no one knew my husband or me. Slowly I felt my heart settle to a semi-reasonable pace and I was able to move one foot in front of the other. My eyes were fixed on my target – the seat next to Tina – I pressed my way forward to my impending doom.

"So!" Tina's words almost made my jewelry jump twice from her skin.

"*So what?*" I responded in a weakened and defeated voice.

"*Sooo…*" Tina continued rubbing my thigh as she bent forward trying to move my eye contact from the floor to hers.

"It will be fine. Don't worry girl. You're

going to go in there, take a test, and the results will be positive – " My already large eyes widened to twice their size. "I mean positive in a negative way – *Oh girl!* You know what I mean." Tina quickly corrected.

"Tina, I'm scared. I mean like I'm praying for death scared." I spoke like there was no on left in the room. The walls felt like a Catholic confessional and this was my last chance to tell all my worst fears to a priest because I was convinced that it was safer to have a buffer between God and me. "I've really fucked up this time. How did I manage to do all the things I spent my whole life avoiding? I don't want to face tomorrow. Hell! I don't even want to face the next five minutes! God left me a long time ago…or maybe I left HIM. Either way somebody left somebody and now the suffering begins. I can't even pray for forgiveness. What's the point when the punishment is this or worse? No human being can handle this all on their own. FUCK MY LIFE!" I shouted! "FUCK MY LIFE! Fuck it all! I'm getting out of here and never looking back! I'm ready to run –" My words became so conscious and slow. I never noticed the tears and sympathy in Tina's eyes and on a few other waiting room patrons. "Runaway from it all. I'm too scared to commit suicide so what now? Disappear? That's what I'll do. Just disappear." I continued.

I lifted my depressed eyes filled with solid tears that fell like pebbles from my round cheeks. "I don't want to know," I said as I rose from my chair. Suddenly I felt Tina's warm touch on my arm and I froze.

"You have to know. For your own sake, you have to. I can't imagine how this feels but – you have to! Now sit your ass back down in this chair and wait for them to call your name." With each word Tina's voice went from sympathy to stern. I dropped down into the seat again.

"By the way your name is Sheba, just one name, like Cher," Tina smirked. "I wanted to make sure you were registered and just in case you ran into someone…well you know."

"Sheba, huh." I shook my head and took what felt like the longest sip of water on the planet. "Sheba! Sheba! Really?!" we laughed.

"So obviously you didn't tell J.J. but how far along do you think you are?" Tina asked. "I mean it can't be that far, ya'll just madeup."

"Tina, one thing I don't need the doctor to tell me is who this baby belongs to. James and I haven't had sex in a long time." I looked at her. "This is Raymond's baby."

"WHAT!" Tina screamed.

"*Shhh!* Keep your voice down. What's wrong with you!" I hit her leg.

"Desiree! How can this be Ray's baby? Oh, wait! This happened in Florida?" Tina asked.

"That could be one answer. It depends on how far along I am."

"Desiree!" She said my name again. "Are you trying to tell me that you've had sex with Ray after we came back from Florida?" Tina interrogated me.

"Yes. That's exactly what I'm saying. I

broke it off a few days ago." I confessed.

"A few days ago!" Tina's shrieks increased.

"Why are you so upset? I'm the one in the predicament, remember?"

Before Tina could answer a nurse called, "Sheba. Is there a Sheba in the waiting room?" I stood and walked to the back like a lamb to slaughter.

"I took a blood test and I am pregnant." My voice was weak. "What are we going to do now?" A long silence followed.

"I don't know. I – what do you want to do?"

"Why don't you be a man for once and open your fat mouth and say what you want Ray!" I screamed into the phone.

"I don't want to have a baby right now."

"Just say it already!"

"I want you to get rid of it," Ray said in a matter of fact tone.

"Thank you! Thank you for finally being honest."

Silence.

"I'm not ready for a baby right now. We aren't even in a relationship. I have too much shit going on and this isn't making it any better." Ray finally added.

"You're not ready….You're-not-ready! What the fuck do you think I'm going through? You're an ass!" I screamed in a low desperate voice.

"Why don't you tell me how you really feel," Raymond said sarcastically.

"You bastard! You don't want to know how I really feel. I don't think I should even speak the things I really want to say to you." My resentment was apparent.

Silence.

"You know what, I *will* tell you what I think of you right now – I wish I never met you! I'm pissed off at myself for ever allowing you into my life. I knew you were 'that guy' but I kept trying to believe that you weren't. That was a big mistake. I wish I could take this all back! I wish you were never born. I wish I never trusted you! I'm kicking myself for even believing in you! You are a bastard and a bitch. And that is just the tip of the iceberg. You don't want me to continue!" I was holding back tears because I didn't want to show any more vulnerability. I took a deep breath and let out a simple sigh.

Silence.

"I'll talk to you later." Ray finally responded. Click.

I'd been taken advantage of by the first person I ever felt comfortable enough to be fully free with. I sat on the porch and cried for what seemed like hours. Too disoriented to make any sudden moves I stared at the sky praying for direction. I prayed that GOD would take the time to save me from myself. The thought of killing a child because that asshole was not man enough to handle what we'd created was too much. "He just threw me away. Just like that." I snapped my fingers. Now I had to find a way to tell my husband about this little situation.

Tina was livid that Ray was involved with me but only because she felt she was the better choice for him. And because she knew she would lose in the end if Raymond had to make a choice between the two of us. She'd come to the conclusion that she had to stack the deck in her favor.

"Excuse me, Mr. Taylor, you have a guest." James' administrative assistant buzzed.

"I'm a little busy right now, who is it?" James asked.

"Tina Harper. She says it's important."

Tina had never come to his office before, *this must be urgent*, James thought. "Send her in." Tina entered his office and took a seat. "What can I help you with?" James asked suspiciously.

"I will get straight to the point. Your wife is pregnant and it's not yours. I just thought you should know." Tina said with disdain.

"What did you just say?" James couldn't believe his ears.

"You heard me," Tina said standing up. "Get your house in order!" She walked out the door.

James swallowed hard and loosened his tie. He felt light headed and picked up his coffee mug and threw it across the room.

During the week James apologized and I tried to get a hold of Ray, I spent every free moment video chatting, texting, talking or fucking J.J. Every morning James sent a text message saying, "Good morning." And although Ray refused to return my calls, Ray would one up him by sending one as well saying, "Good morning beautiful. Have a great day!" followed by a separate naked picture of himself. I had so many pictures of Ray's lickable nude body I could have created an entire library of Play Girl. I kept them for a few hours then deleted the evidence. I never sent any of myself for fear that they'd be used against me later. I did enjoy these little digital reminders of how much I was wanted from both men. I didn't realize how much I was attracted to the excitement of it all until one day Ray didn't respond to me at all.

I went about my day as normal except for incessantly looking at my phone and checking my email. I couldn't concentrate, so I decided to go to a movie to get my mind off of things. I picked up the phone and dialed Tina's phone number. No answer. I dialed Ray once more, again, no answer. For some reason, I desperately needed attention, so I dialed J.J.'s number. No answer. *Where the hell was everybody?* I dialed Tina again and left a voice message. "Hey, Tina! It's Desiree, call me as soon as you get this message. I'm having a really weird problem and I could use my friend right now."

Now let's be clear about this. I wasn't misguided about what was going on between Ray and me, it had nothing to do with love, even though he always seemed to make that the case. I didn't fall for it, at first, because he was so good at being deceitful. He was quick on his feet when it came to lying or covering up what was going on and I promised myself not to get my feelings involved. This whole situation was wrong but every time I tried to talk myself out of it, Ray talked me back into it. Tina and Ray were good at that, or maybe I was too gullible. Either way, I knew the consequences. Like I said, playing this game means sacrificing your own heart as a casualty, and mine just became a casualty. By all accounts, I was still in love with my estranged husband. I really did want to work things out with the man I married, but I wasn't sure if he'd ever wake up and realize that there were so many things we needed to fix.

Frustrated, I loaded myself into my car and drove down the avenue where I spotted my favorite smoothie stand. I pulled to the curb and ordered my regular mango strawberry drink. I took a few sips and dawdled my way back to the car. I looked across the street and noticed Ray beeping his horn and pulling into a parking spot in front of a boutique. I waved and called out to him, but he didn't hear me. I made a move toward him when I froze in my tracks. Walking out of the boutique and up to Raymond's car was Tina and the girl I'd had the ménage with! I dropped my cup in disbelief. I couldn't believe my eyes! My heart started to pound in my ears and I heard ringing. I looked around for someone to notice that I needed help, but no one came to my aide. As the pair piled into Ray's car, he pulled away from the curb. They never noticed me. I was utterly invisible – I must have been. There I was losing my entire mind and no one was there to help me.

I sprinted back to my car and sped away. I had no idea where I was going or what I was going to do. All I could think about is how and why this is happening to me. I was smarter than this! The emotional wreck status that had begun the moment I saw my best friend with my lover seemed to increase every two to three minutes like contractions. I fell for it! I fell for a...a...a womanizer that didn't see anything wrong with gallivanting around town with my best friend! In that moment, everything I thought I ever wanted from him was gone. I looked at him differently.

Ray was the epitome of calculated tenderness just for the effect of it. You know, the mind trips people play just to fuck with you...give you just enough affection to cloud your mind and make you believe in whatever they're selling....Just enough for you not to suspect what they're doing. This game is *not* for the faint of heart.

I felt sick to my stomach when it finally sunk in – he'd been having a new affair with her ex-best friend for months now. It all started to make sense. The phone calls trying to make sure that she stayed away at times. How Tina always lets me know that she'd seen Ray here or there. Or making sure I knew how much Tina needed me as a friend. All this time I questioned why Ray was on Tina's side all of a sudden. *Back stabbing tramp!* Thoughts raced through my head like an Indi-500 race. I sank to the floor holding my stomach wishing I could take it all back. *It's Too late now!* Too much damage had already been done. How could I ever believe that he could love me and be faithful when our whole relationship began with a lie. "This is my hell on earth." The realization that it meant nothing at all slapped me in the face. They won! I was beaten to the floor with no hope of getting up. *How did this happen to me? How? I always had it so together.* "He looked me right in my eyes and fed me that shit and I believed every word." I pounded the floor.

"I told him this was too intense! I warned him that we won't be able to take any of this back!" I screamed.

I dialed his number hoping to get all of this out of my system. I held my belly on the cold white ceramic tiled floor she felt a painful jab, my cries became screams. I grabbed myself tighter and suddenly felt wet. I looked at my feet she noticed a crimson stain spreading over my thigh high pink baby doll dress. "Oh my GOD!!! Oh, my GOD!!! GOD, please help me!!!"

I could no longer move, the pain took my breath away. Death would be a welcome phase of life right now. Now was as good a time as any other. Another jab. I didn't reach for the phone as I stared at the legs of the kitchen table from the ground up. *Jab. Jab. Jab. Jab.* I quietly cried. There was no need to scream anymore...no need for anything...just the painful death that I deserved. Another jab. "Oooouch!" she whispered as she slipped in and out of consciousness. *Jab. Jab. Jab.*

All the shame that I felt, all the guilt I thought had gone came rushing back and I suddenly couldn't breathe any longer. The light floors started to spin again and the light breaking through the window shades became so bright – extremely bright. I let out a small sigh.

"Oh my God!" he shouted. "Wake up! Please wake up!"

I'd never felt tears on my face that were so cold before. They were cold like ice rolling down my cheek then to my chin and off to the side. It gave me chills.

"Forgive me. Please forgive me." I said faintly. "I loved you. I'm so sorry."

"You can't leave me. I know it's selfish, but you are supposed to be here with me. You are supposed to be here to get mad at me and cuss me out and tell me I'm special. You are supposed to be here! This is not fair. You can't do this!" More cold tears down my face but these were not my tears. These tears belonged to him.

NOTHING BUT THE RIGHTEOUS

I woke up early that Sunday morning. I lay in bed for hours thinking about what it was that I really wanted in life. I kept questioning why I'd never taken the time to introduce James to who I was becoming. You see, the truth about deception is it's very broad. It is easier to deceive someone when you don't think of your actions as being deceptive. And then there are lies we tell ourselves, in the end, it appears that we can't handle the truth at all. As the ceiling fan rotated overhead, I lost myself in a muted prayer. It was time for me to return to church. I needed answers and direction and I wasn't going to get any of that laying in bed. I got up and showered then made my way to the church house. I got there just in time for the scripture reading;

"Even if I should choose to boast, I would not be a fool, because I would be speaking the truth. But I refrain so no one will think more of me than is warranted by what I do or say, or because of these surpassingly great revelations. Therefore, in order to keep me from becoming conceited, I was given a thorn in my flesh, a messenger of Satan, to torment

me. Three times I pleaded with the Lord to take it away from me. But he said to me, "My grace is sufficient for you, for my power is made perfect in weakness." Therefore I will boast all the more gladly about my weaknesses, so that Christ's power may rest on me. That is why, for Christ's sake, I delight in weaknesses, in insults, in hardships, in persecutions, in difficulties. For when I am weak, then I am strong." (2 Corinthians 12: 6-10)

Shortly after I arrived, James sat on the steps of the church, lost in thought, thinking about all the things that could have gone wrong from what he'd just discovered. He blamed himself and rationalized that this was GOD punishing him for his infidelity. He heard the choir singing and got up the courage to enter the large oak doors to face his demons. As he pressed his way into the sanctuary, the pastor had opened the doors of the church and asked if anyone needed prayer.

I sat still as I watched my husband drag his body up the center of the aisle each step more labored than the last. I had no idea he was even in the building. He took a seat next to the church clerk on the first bench and whispered something in her ear. She shook her head in agreement and asked him to stand before the church. "Brother Taylor would like to address the congregation," she said handing my husband the microphone.

"I just want to thank you all for the years of love and support you've shown my beloved wife and I over the past few years. It is with a heavy heart that I come to you today asking forgiveness and understanding for a very delicate situation. I'm angry and hurt and unsure of what to do next." He took a deep breath and sniffled.

"Son, you don't have to give us specifics, GOD already knows." The pastor said covering the top of the microphone to dull the sound.

"No pastor, I have to do this." J.J. continued. "I was unfaithful to my wife. To the only woman, I've ever truly loved." He said breaking down. "I thought I could hide it. I thought I would get through it on my own....But I guess GOD had another plan for me because....because...I found out my whore of a wife got me back! Yes, she did!"

The pastor tried to pry the microphone from his cold hands and the church started an uproar of chatter and accusations."Brother Taylor! This is not the place -"

"Not the place for what Pastor? For honesty? For repenting? I thought this was the right place! I guess that's my punishment, huh! All of my business is in the streets and I had to hear it from the man that – her adulterer! I know what I did was wrong, but she didn't have to do that to me! She didn't! I didn't deserve that! No man deserves that." He shouted falling to his knees. "If I'm going to be publicly humiliated then I will be damned if she is going to walk out of here the unscathed perfect wife!" The church ushers scrambled to cut the sound from the microphones, but his voice carried throughout the high acoustic ceilings and into the ears of each and every member.

My heart stopped. I couldn't breathe nor could I stand. I dropped down in the pew with my hand over my mouth in total disbelief. I couldn't even cry. I searched the room for an escape, forgetting that one was directly to my right. I frantically searched again for a forgiving face among the on-lookers. No one looked trustworthy or even remotely in the likeness of Jesus. So I did the next best thing, I ran to the front of the church and plead my case.

"This is no one's business but ours, but my husband is not the victim here! I am! This is what happens when you neglect your wife! When you lie and cheat on your wife, James! Were you all paying attention? He cheated on me first! It's not for any of you to judge him or me or our marriage." I said kicking J.J., who was still on his knees on the floor. "I'm not perfect! I never claimed to be! That was you all that put me in that place. I never asked or even wanted to be there! So to all you judgmental saints in these pews this morning you need to look at yourself first before you start trying to correct my house!" I took a breath. "I love my husband and I love my family. I made a mistake."

"You loved him so much you slept with another man instead of making your man happy." A voice came from the audience.

"Actually, if you *must* know, I slept with another man and woman after trying to work it out with a man that betrayed me first!" I corrected the female spectator.

"You see! This is what happens when you put your trust in man." The voice said coming closer.

There stood Tina. My supposedly best friend in the entire world was personally giving me a scarlet letter. Our eyes met and locked. She folded her hands across her chest and the pastor prevented her from coming one step closer. They must have been more afraid of her coming after me than my reaction to her. While the Deacons rushed to stop her from continuing this spectacle any longer, they forgot about me. I was pulling off my shoes and earrings. When I felt the last dangle of my earring escape from my finger, I took off like Muhammad Ali in a welterweight fight. I landed three fists to her eye before one of the deaconesses could pull my shoulder back. This proved to be a mistake because that allowed me enough room to miss her swing. My fist went all the way back to Egypt and landed right at her address! I regained control of my shoulder and land three more blows to her face. I was careful not to hit anyone but my target. Tina was still wildly swinging when the congregation, including James, was able to put some distance between us. J.J. made sure to release any hold he was able to get on me before I turned around.

"You!" I screamed. "How dare you!"

"I'm sorry. This is all my fault." He cried. "I'm sorry," He said again as I pushed past him and walked to the outer pews toward the exit. Barefoot and emotionless I busted through the doors of the church and sprinted toward my car.

"Sister Taylor! Sister Taylor, please come back inside. The devil is busy! We can't let you leave like this." The first lady shouted after me. I didn't want to hear anything else, so I kept walking and she stopped chasing. I climbed into my SUV and locked the doors, but I didn't put the keys in the ignition. The whole scene was something out of a movie. This couldn't be my life right now! How could it? I know plenty of people in this very church that have done way worse and they are looking down their noses at me?! This is not how I wanted to discuss this with my husband. This is not how I wanted this to end. Tina had big nerve! I've never believed in jealousy but with friends like her you don't need enemies. This was too much betrayal for one lifetime.

THOSE NECESSARY THORNS

I love GOD! I love Jesus! Yet I'm confused about what I am supposed to be doing. I know that HE will direct my path and in all ways acknowledge HIM yada yada yada. I am confused about my friends, my enemies, my love life, my life period. I decided that I can't play the game anymore. I want out. I don't know what I need. I don't even know if I need to cry, scream, sulk, or just stare at the wall. I do know I need to talk to YOU. I have all of these thoughts about all of this and I wonder what I did? What I did to get to this point. Then I remember Pastor's sermon. There is an old adage that says you should be grateful and extremely blessed if you have just ONE true friend on earth. I am not saddened by losing....I'm just trying to understand what is happening in my life. At this point, I am not close to anyone. I feel like I'm missing something.

It was an experience that I won't forget. An experience that I won't regret but something I definitely won't ever do again. We can't keep looking back and wondering what if. Just move on. I'm glad James is happy with his wife and spending time focusing on us. I can't say I wish it were me in his position because I don't. I eliminated Raymond from any position of importance and he didn't like that. For him, leaving me in the cold was punishment but for me it was the best thing he could have ever done. He showed me who he really was. It made me deal with all the emotions and things that went on between us and I didn't need any of it. It wasn't worth it. He wasn't worth it. Whatever *"it"* is just wasn't worth it. It helped me see. "Three times I pleaded with the Lord to take it away from me. But he said to me, "My grace is sufficient for you, for my power is made perfect in weakness." I was happy to say I was delivered from *"it"*…from him.

After all was said and done, I feel good. Not about the things I've done but about the way we left them. You know how sometimes when things end someone always feels as though they lost. Well, in this case, I think we won! Our relationship has changed for the better. I have never felt so alive, so awake and so loved. We are friends – still friends. Sometimes you have to lose to win again.

That's my story….My testimony. The bathroom of my church basement freed my soul. I splashed more water on my face and patted it dry. When I walked out, James was waiting for me. He offered me his hand and I accepted. We walked up the stairs and out the door.

"Sometimes you remember a week for your whole life," He said.

"Just a week?" I smiled sweetly and looked into his eyes.

"Sometimes you have to realize that this thing was bigger than you or me. Not me and you." He pulled me close and commanded my head on his shoulder.

"How is it that – I mean, I just needed to take the time to get myself together," I answered.

"You just don't know what you do to me." He squeezed me tight.

"And just what do I do to you?" I asked.

"*Hmm*...." He smiled and kissed my forehead. "I loved you when I walked out that door. I never stopped." James Jones Taylor confessed.

If love is a battlefield and we all get scars;These were my reminders...my necessary thorns.

ABOUT THE AUTHOR

Sabrina Childress-Miller is a graduate of Columbia College in Chicago, Illinois. Armed with a degree in Marketing Communications, Sabrina has managed a dual career in corporate America and the Not-For-Profit arena through the founding of Position of Pressure, a grassroots domestic violence organization for teens and young adults.

Often described as a paradigm shift, Sabrina left her corporate position to pursue a career in writing. Working on a book about the struggles, temptations, and triumphs of relationships, perceptions, and expectations; challenging others to deal with the real issues of being human. This pursuit evolved into *Those Necessary Thorns*, a fictional book series. It is her first book. Sabrina lives in Chicago with her husband.